MAQUISARD

In the memory,
in the heart:
stones live...

1998
For Tuve
M/Juutti/M

Other books by ALBERT J. GUERARD

Fiction

The Past Must Alter

The Hunted

Night Journey

The Bystander

The Exiles

Christine/Annette

Gabrielle

The Hotel in the Jungle

Nonfiction

Robert Bridges

Joseph Conrad

Thomas Hardy

André Gide

Conrad the Novelist

The Triumph of the Novel: Dickens, Dostoevsky, Faulkner

The Touch of Time: Myth, Memory and the Self

MAQUISARD

A Christmas Tale

by

Albert J. Guerard

LYFORD
Books

The characters, events, and military situations described in this novel are fictitious.

Published by Presidio Press
505 B San Marin Drive, Suite 300
Novato, CA 94945-1340

Library of Congress Cataloging-in-Publication Data

Guérard, Albert J. (Albert Joseph), 1914–
Maquisard : a Christmas tale / Albert J. Guerard.
p. cm.
ISBN 0-89141-585-8
1. World War, 1939-1945—France—Cognac—Fiction. 2. Christmas—France—Cognac—Fiction. 3. Christmas stories, American.
I. Title.
PS3513.U353M37 1995
813'.52—dc20 95-34781
CIP

Printed in the United States of America

For

Eric Solomon

who encouraged all my fictions

Author's Note

Maquisard: A Christmas Tale is based on a few weeks in December 1944 I spent with French forces in Cognac in southwest France. They were stationed near the Royan coastal "pocket" (the "Orillan" of the novel), a garrison left behind by the Germans when they retreated after the fall of Normandy and Brittany. The French mission was to liquidate the garrison or at least prevent it from breaking out to occupy more French cities.

My novel, closely based on experience, is an affectionate recollection of a number of persons who met every day in a small cafe, where they huddled over the wood stove and drank cognac to shut out the cold and shut out too the traumatic memories of friends and families, wives and children lost or imprisoned, tortured or killed by the German occupier.

Most of the French soldiers in Cognac were members of the resistance army FFI *(Forces Françaises de l'Interieur).* Many of them had previously been in guerrilla brigades of the FTP *(Francs Tireurs et Partisans Français).* They had fought in the *maquis* ("thorny bush"), engaged in sabotage, derailing trains and otherwise harassing the enemy—hence *maquisard.* My fictional Lieutenant Colvin was an OSS (Office of Strategic Services) officer who had been parachuted to the maquis in 1943.

An Afterword explains more fully the military and political situation. A Glossary is appended to clarify a few unfamiliar terms.

MAQUISARD

Chapter I

The news quickly went the length and depth of the small front held by the Ruc Brigade: arms were arriving at last. After four months of their waiting, a truck had come that very afternoon, hauling behind it an American .155. The good news traveled as fast as though it were bad, reaching every outpost on the fifteen miles of marshy front before two hours had passed. The courier bringing mail from headquarters at Sognac stopped at each farmhouse on the Orillan road to tell the machine gunners watching from the attics, whose job was to defend that road. He had seen the .155 himself; it would arrive in Rujon that day. The last farmhouse, after which the road straightened out for seven miles of waste no-man's-land, relayed the news to the advance posts three and four hundred yards ahead: six-man slit trenches dug out of the frozen earth. And from this same farmhouse the news fanned north and south — south to the tiny village of St. Pierre-de-Marennes, from which the suburbs of Orillan itself could be seen; north to the marshy promontory of Trulac, a spit that was neither sea nor land. Here the Germans were less than a kilometer away, just across the river; and on certain nights, when there was no sound from the sea, you could hear the stamping and the talk of the enemy's advance patrols. They were harsh strange voices, and the men were presumed to be Poles. But more often these enemy patrols were silent and invisible, like the French patrols that edged out on to the river itself to observe them, on flat-bottomed boats propelled by long poles, two men to a boat.

The first reaction to the news was nearly always the same. The very words were the same: "Sans blague!" or "I don't believe it," or "It's about time!" The men would look at each other and then down at their own weapons, which had stood them during eighteen months in the maquis and four months of holding this particular pocket of Germans left behind: the small brassy Spanish pistols and the hunting rifles, or the occasional parachuted British sub-machine gun, useless at over fifty yards. And they tried to imagine what it would be like to fight a war with decent arms. An American .155! Some at once talked learnedly of this gun — its velocity, range, and power to destroy; as usual, to avoid freezing, they hopped up and down as they talked. But since they had come directly to the coast from the maquis, and had never been in the American sector north of the Loire, none of them had seen one of the guns. Through the afternoon the adjudants in charge of each post allowed one man at a time to go back to Rujon and see the .155.

They found it in the garage behind the Regimental C.P., guarded proudly by four men. It was still covered by its green camouflage net, but the long barrel pointed unmistakably toward the back of the truck. They lifted a corner of the net and stroked its clean black sides. They would have liked to waken the driver who had brought the truck and the gun, a French soldier in green American fatigues, now sleeping in the heated kitchen. They had a hundred questions to ask him. But they waited patiently for him to sleep himself out. They all assumed that if one American .155 had come, there would be many others; there would even be uniforms and shoes for all.

On land it was nearly dark at five o'clock. On the river, or at the doubtful point where the river merged with the marshy land, the evening fog had swirled in. Even the boat patrol, Jean Ruyader and René Pleyel, had heard the news: they talked about it in whispers as they inched north toward the Point, poling along cautiously behind the last high reeds. They changed places every twenty minutes, but now Jean sat at the prow with the field-glasses, the rifle, and the bottle of cognac. René stood at the back of the boat; he leaned his weight on the pole to push the boat on, feeling for solid ground and then pulling away from the mud. They were wet through, though there was no rain but the fog, and every five minutes or so they took a short drink from the bottle. Even when Jean talked he kept looking through the glasses, which they had taken from the last batch of German prisoners. Usually he could see nothing beyond the reeds. But the fog came and went intermittently, like gusts of rain, and from time to time the opposite shore appeared. Right now, he couldn't see a thing.

Jean, who had been in an artillery division in 1940, told René as much as he knew about heavy pieces, such as the American .155. But what he knew was very little, since his regiment had never received its equipment. It had been activated in May, only in time to join the general southern retreat along the choked Poitiers road. From Poitiers, at the time of the Armistice, he had profited by the first confusion to go to the farm of his wife's parents near Auxerre. But he was not to remain there long.

René gave the pole a long angry push.

"What good's the gun, if we don't know how to use it? We're all veterans – veterans who know how to clean a Luger or cock a stem-gun! Or maybe blow up a bridge. What the devil are we going to do with a .155?"

"You're right," Jean said. "And suppose there's not just one .155? Suppose there's fifty of them?"

"Maybe Colonel Ruc knows — "

"Colonel Ruc! Do you know what he was in 1940? A captain in something called Chemical Warfare. Gases and mines and all that stuff. I bet he can't tell a .155 from a .105."

René looked at him in surprise. "Are you crazy? There wasn't a better leader in any maquis."

"I know. I'm not saying anything against him. I'm just saying he doesn't know anything about a .155. You have to be a specialist. You have to be in artillery to know something about it."

René edged the boat ahead with one more long push. Then he pulled the pole aboard and let the boat coast ahead till it stopped, the prow just touching the last thin line of reeds. This was as far as they could go without turning inshore or out on to the open water. It was less than half a mile to the opposite shore and the nearest enemy post. But now the space between was hung with a curtain that was almost rain: cold wet fog sucked down to meet and swirl with mist sucked up from the sea. René sat down and rolled a cigarette, though he would not be able to light it until they returned to land.

"The Americans wouldn't have sent us a .155 if we couldn't use it. They don't give things away as easy as that."

"You're telling me! But they don't always know what they're doing, the Americans. Remember how they dropped us machine guns but no ammunition? Another time it was batteries but no transmitter. Even the Americans can get things tangled up." Jean clapped his gloves together sharply. "But of course! Tommy can teach us how to use them. He'll know about .155's. Maybe he knew all along the .155's were coming, and that's why he stuck with us."

Tommy was Lieutenant Thomas Colvin, an American who had been parachuted to the maquis in August 1943, to collect intelligence on the secret army. And he was to be on hand to teach them how to use a new plastic in blowing up bridges, and how to fire bazookas—should these things ever be sent. He had been with them ever since. The plastics arrived safely in December, but the first bazookas, brought over in the spring of 1944, fell directly in the path of a small German patrol. Night after night, and finally week and week, they waited for more bazookas. But none ever came.

René looked skeptically into the fog.

"I doubt it. I know for a fact that he was supposed to go home in August—at least for a furlough, perhaps to be demobilized. He doesn't know any more about .155's than you or I. He knows about plastics. And bazookas."

"Bazookas!" Jean spat into the water. *"Merde!"*

When he looked up again the fog had rolled away. He realized now that the glasses had been entirely out of focus. The curtain folded away on both sides to leave a widening cone of light, and across the eight hundred yards of water the opposite shore shelved up in a thin black line. A single rifle shot crackled, far beyond the shack. In the intense silence they could hear the sound of the bolt pulled back.

"They saw us?"

"It's impossible. We're completely covered. They can't see a thing. Besides, it came from beyond the shack."

Jean followed the widening horizon with his field-glasses. In the thin fog half a mile to the south the yellow headlights of a car glared for a moment and were gone.

The glasses picked out the bare details from this point to the shack: marshy reeds and an occasional scrabble of black rocks. A small colony of gulls had settled on one of these rocks, and there were smaller birds beyond. There was no one near the shack. But farther to the north, at the extreme point of land where the German pocket ended, he could see the lighthouse and the flat quicksand. He looked away quickly from that brown waste, out of which the shards and spars of three small boats still protruded. Before the war the lighthouse had warned ships away, but now the Germans left it dark. The three ships, however, had been there for many years, marking the depth of the sands. Dozens of men, even hundreds perhaps, had been sucked under there — tourists, vacationers who knew no better. He could imagine their bodies mingled with the ripped skeletons of the ships. They were the strongest quicksands in France.

"Let me have the glasses," René said. He focused them quickly; then he looked away from them. "You know? It's just possible we're all going to be relieved."

"Relieved?"

"Listen, I said it's just possible. They might be sending down the regular army. A real American division. Or even a French one. I've wondered all along why Tourelle was here. A three-star general!"

Relieved. At first it was only the word. Jean could not think of himself as anywhere except on this front, in this dank cold mist, on this flat-bottomed boat.

"You're crazy. Maybe they'll send us some supplies. But as for being relieved — "

"Do you know what that might mean?" René went on eagerly. "Paris for Christmas. I wouldn't know my way around the Métro, after five years."

"Forget about it."

"And you could see your brats, Jean. You could be with them for Christmas."

"Shut up!" Jean said sharply.

But there it was. He had thought of that at once, as soon as he had taken in the word. A year and a half old. Four, seven, and nine. It was Milou, now a year and a half, he most wanted to see. Because he had never seen him; had learned of his existence only four months ago, when he learned also of his wife's death. Milou was born in July 1943; two months later his wife was shot as a hostage, one of seven women in the village to die that day.

"Don't you want to see them? It would be just right if you could get there for Christmas Eve."

"They wouldn't know me — even Denise, although she's already nine. They're better off not seeing me. They may not even know about their mother."

"Shh!" René whispered.

They listened. Far down the bay there was the unmistakable sound of a motorboat: the German patrol. Jean tested the safety of his rifle, and they squatted far down in the boat. Now that they could hear the boat coming, there were also other sounds: the drone of a plane, their own breathing, a sea-mew's melancholy cry. The boat — a twenty-foot speedboat — appeared abruptly out of the fog to their left, in the very middle of the channel. A 50-millimeter machine gun was mounted on the prow; behind it crouched a German in Kriegsmarine uniform. The boat was going about fifteen miles an hour.

"It's like everything else," René whispered. "They've got armored cars; we've got broken-down Citroëns. They've got .88's; we've got pistols. Even for patrolling they've got the very best."

"Shut up!" Jean said aloud. "Shut up and keep down and don't move!"

For as he watched the boat go to the Point and then circle back down the channel, to cross them again, he was thinking of his four children in the kitchen of his mother-in-law's farm near Auxerre. And beyond that — his whole body tightening slowly under him, irresistibly gathering itself in — he was trying for one more time to see what had happened: to see his wife, terrified and screaming, standing against a wall.

He edged himself forward on his elbows until the rifle rested on the flat cover of the prow. The patrol boat was almost opposite now. He slipped his finger under the trigger guard.

"What the hell are you doing?" René asked sharply.

"That!" The gun barked; and then the shot was echoing far over the water and the land. Almost at once they saw the machine gun on the prow of the patrol boat swing over toward them; and they heard the motor slow. The flock of small birds sprayed drunkenly away from the rocks and then screamed as they carilloned upward; the gulls scattered more slowly.

"You fool!" René said. "You God-damned fool!"

They lay down with their faces against the wet planks. A moment later they heard the first thin whistle and then the spattering of the machine-gun bullets against the water and the reeds. They were landing fifty or a hundred yards south; the sound of the bullets on the water and the reeds was like buckshot against a wall. There was a burst of fifteen or twenty rounds; then silence and another twenty rounds.

"You could get court-martialed for this. You could get months in prison. Years."

"I'm sorry," Jean said. "I had to do it."

"Well, it's the last time I go out on a patrol with you. You're trigger-happy. You don't know what you're doing."

"I guess I don't."

René inched forward and touched Jean's shoulder. "It's all right," he said very slowly. "It was just such a damned fool thing to do."

There were no more shots. For perhaps five minutes they heard the idling motor of the patrol boat; it was out in the middle of the channel, waiting like a living thing for them to give some sign. Then it picked up speed and went on down the channel. But it might come back. They kept down with their faces against the bottom of the boat, and they began to taste the salt on the wet planks. At last there was no sound at all. They sat up then; it was nearly dark.

There was nothing more to see; already, the opposite shore had disappeared. Jean took the pole and worked the boat around toward shore. He was very wet now, and he could see nothing ahead but the dark water and the wet reeds. The fog and the cold closed in.

Back at the Regimental Command Post in Rujon, they knew it was not merely a question of getting arms at last. The whole unit was to be relieved. At least the officers at the C.P. — the Hôtel de France et de la Charente — knew it. The Bretagne division which had stormed into Alsace was coming down to finish the job. It was to be supported by a fresh division of motorized Spahis. Captain Morel had been at General Tourelle's headquarters that morning; and there were others, returning from a few days in Paris, who had seen the great convoy on the road, fifty kilometers of trucks, tanks, and jeeps. At Sognac even the parasites and hangers-on to every major operation had begun to arrive: the British and American liaison officers and the correspondents. It would be a kind of vacation for the Bretagne division, superbly equipped, to move up the

Atlantic coast, reducing the enemy pockets one by one: Orillan, La Pallice, La Rochelle. St. Nazaire and Lorient were tough nuts to crack, but by that time the division would be rested, after such an easy campaign. As for the Ruc Brigade, it had done its job well, but it was not trained for motorized war. It decidedly needed a rest.

The officers themselves were tired. With relief in sight, the first artillery piece having arrived as a token, they gave in at last to fatigue. Only a few recent arrivals (such as Lieutenant Jantal, who had joined the Brigade late in November after fifty months' imprisonment near Aachen) were sorry to leave. They huddled near the stoves through the cold December afternoon, silent and exhausted, sleepily debating whether they would be home in time for Christmas. Now that the years of guerrilla fighting were over, and the months of nervously guarding the Orillan pocket, they wondered for the first time at their own endurance: how they had stood it so long. They thought sleepily of their families and home.

It had been something of a comic-opera war since late in August, when the Germans who did not surrender or make for Belfort or Spain retreated to the coastal ports. Before that it had been anything but a comic-opera war. During the three years the Brigade had known every kind of guerrilla action, and every kind of success. In August 1941, numbering forty-five men, they burned a dozen German trucks with bottles of gasoline; in that first month they were still working in cells, and they did not know each other. In July of 1944 only seven of the original forty-five had not been killed, but these seven had been joined by four thousand others, and in that month they blew up or derailed a train every day, almost completely paralyzing the Paris-Bordeaux line. Road bridges, radio stations, telephone wires, even a large munitions dump –

the successful year culminated in the capture of two major cities after pitched battles with the Germans. They had begun as isolated cells, and then in December of 1942 as a tiny and unnamed maquis in the mountains of the Dordogne. But soon they were officially attached to the Franc-Tireurs et Partisans, the quasi-communist F.T.P. After the liberation they were absorbed once more, through the nation-wide agreement, by the French Forces of the Interior, the F.F.I. – and, as a last step in this slow and reluctant metamorphosis, by the French Army itself. In the three years each of the seven survivors had been wounded (*Adjudant-chef* Ruyader eight times), and Captain Ruc had been appointed full colonel by Paris headquarters of the F.T.P. Now back in the army, he was allowed to keep his rank. But some of his officers, such as Ruyader, lacked the necessary educational qualifications and were reduced to *adjudant-chef*. Tommy Colvin, who went up to Paris in the last days of August to get uniformed, was quietly amused to find that in his long absence from the American Army he had become a first lieutenant.

It had been a comic-opera war during these four months because the Germans in Orillan were content to stay there quietly, controlling the river mouth. The Ruc Brigade, with a few Citroëns and Peugeots to send against armored cars and even a few tanks, was far too weak to attack. At best they could merely stand guard, or file intelligence reports – reports to the effect that the Germans could at any moment, if they wanted, break out and retake Angoulême or Bordeaux. The Germans did break out from time to time, some armored cars followed by trucks, to forage a few miles of countryside for food. On these occasions the Brigade was obliged to retreat. They could merely harass the enemy column with grenades and light machine-gun fire. Then the Germans interrupted their foraging to hunt out the patrols; and a few men from each side would be killed. Occasionally a strong Brigade patrol worked its way across the mined no-man's-land in the dark, to surprise and capture a German advance post. The prisoners were brought to Rujon for interrogation in German by Colvin and Lieutenant Jantal; and over the four months the Brigade had accumulated enough intelligence to secure an offensive, if ever arms should arrive. It was, nevertheless, a demoralizing, unpleasant little campaign; and dangerous enough, if one accumulated the small losses. It was exhausting because they were undermanned and had no proper clothes for such a climate. Their best protection was an unlimited supply of cognac. There were no men who fought barefoot, but there were few who had good shoes. There were far more casualties from trench-foot and frostbite than from enemy fire. It was chiefly because of this that they were glad to be relieved: the unchanging wet and cold.

Lieutenant Colvin, who had spent the afternoon warming his feet against the tiny stove in the intelligence office, was as glad as anyone else. He would probably have been court-martialed had a G.I. American colonel — say from Civil Affairs or the Transportation Corps — visited the post that afternoon. For very little remained of his agent's uniform, itself so different from the standard officer's issue. He had given his high combat boots to Ruyader and was wearing black low-cut civilian shoes. His field jacket had disappeared in the course of an evening of playing *belote,* and he had on the green blouse of the F.T.P. He had given his fur-lined jacket to Captain Hernandez, who nearly always worked outdoors. There was nothing to distinguish him as an American officer except the gold bar on his French army cap, now worn far back to keep his neck warm. He had not bothered, since returning from Paris in September, to put on his new and shiny silver bar. His tie hung loosely outside his blouse.

So, he thought, *it's over at last!* With the arrival of the Bretagne division he could go home — perhaps for a thirty-day furlough and a soft desk job with the research department in Washington; perhaps even to resume teaching French literature at Princeton. In the last days of August he had gone to Paris to get uniformed (what a statement of charges he would have to sign!) ; they had wanted to send him home. He might not have refused, had he known this small operation would drag on till Christmas. In August and early September Patton's tanks were stabbing across France, encountering almost no resistance. Nancy, Verdun, even perhaps to the Saar. Only pessimists said the war would last till Armistice Day. It was the least he could do, after having been so long with the Brigade — belonging so much more to it than to the American Army — to stay with it, a few more weeks to the end. With his friends sent on this last assignment he could hardly go back to the Princeton campus; or even to the nice clean desks and the secretaries, the electric lights, the warm Washington hotels. There was little for him to do. But he knew that he represented something beyond himself to these men who so absurdly idolized him. There were other maquis, no larger than theirs, that had been sent several agents. But he was the only one who had been sent to the Ruc Brigade, and he had been for many months their only physical reminder of the outside world. On that black endless August night, jumping a few seconds later from the same plane, his French fellow agent and his radio operator, an American sergeant, had been killed.

"Enfin!" he said aloud. He opened the stove grate and put his feet on the ledge. What would it be like to go home? He tried to visualize himself sitting in a department or faculty meeting, listening to the interminable splitting of fine hairs, but he could see himself only in some such absurd uniform as he now wore, conspicuous among the Oxford gray suits. Only three years ago he had walked the streets of Princeton with a briefcase under his arm. But at thirty his life had been made over. He smiled to think of his own purblind innocence at twenty-six or twenty-seven.

He took out his tobacco pouch filled with tiny butts and rolled himself a cigarette. It was one of the things he had learned. But there was so much else he had learned, in the fifteen months in France. For the first time he had seen men living together; that is, unselfishly. It had been by necessity so, for a single disobeyed order or a single act of egotism would have lost them all. Men are not loyal or unselfish by nature; he learned how hard-won these qualities are. So he had learned, too, the flimsiness of certain abstracts, when shuffled by the dark complexity of experience. He had been in a revolution, and could see now the naïveté and incompleteness of most literary revolutionaries. Were they alive, the comments of Holbach, Condorcet, or Rousseau would be as inept as those of the Bordeaux Resistance newspapers. Having forgotten the texts, he yet understood for the first time the authors he had taught. But this was not all. He had also learned, from months of training and then twenty-five months in France, how to kill a man so quickly and so quietly that there was no sound but that of the limp body being turned on the ground. He had even learned to hate.

Lieutenant Jantal often said that peace would be much surer if America had suffered a little; had lived for a few months under the German occupation; had learned to hate. And yet it was perhaps a good thing that there was one country where, except in certain parts of the South, hate was generally unknown. For hate, though purer than meaningless violence or bickering, was more remote from peace. He thought, more simply: It would be good to be home. Drowsing over the little stove, with the dusk drowsing in, Colvin's mind traversed easily the fifteen months of his learning; it wandered ineluctably backward. Where was this home to which he would now return? Was it the almost intact forest that surrounded the house in Houston where he was born: the persimmon tree at the end of the block? Or the lazy Sundays scooping crayfish from the swollen red gutters? There is much to account for between this child and the man who had learned to hate, who could kill with the softness of a child stroking his dog. Home was perhaps the white house and green lawn where he saw himself after his thirteenth year, playing football through the long California afternoons. But also, in this state of almost sleep, home came to mean many things and places where in a proper sense he did not belong — the exile's composite picture of his country: the barber shops and pool parlors and brown-walled Public Libraries; the county fairs and tall elms of New England; the baked clean wide empty streets of an Iowa town. Or was it only, in his drowsy search, that all these things meant peace; an absence of hate?

Now fully asleep, he dreamed of looking through a long house of many rooms for his wife. Each door he tried opened on a bare room exactly like the last; it was an endless house, and had all the doors opened at once before him it would have been like looking into mirrors endlessly reflecting one another. But at last he came to a door behind which, he knew, she would be. The door opened before he had touched it, and there she was — not exactly as he had left her, but changed; certainly a little older.

For she must have longed for him too. Home, being an abstract, remains always behind some unopened door. But in the eternal absence of this abstract, the heart can find a home.

The sound of the door opening and closing woke him up. Lieutenant Jantal walked over to the stove a little shakily and held his hands over the fire. His regular army uniform was faded to a brown sheen from six years' wear, two in the army and four in the Offlag. He had escaped early in November, and had been quietly drunk ever since. He had walked from Hamund to Valenciennes in the mud, against the American convoys, in his first days of liberty. Under that freezing rain and spattered by the passing trucks he had kept himself half drunk to shut out the cold. He found this condition so pleasant – the sense of things wandering by you, rather than you by them – that he didn't stop drinking, even after reaching Rujon. He was forty-two, round-faced, almost bald. He looked like a man who was trying to fill out his clothes. But putting his hands over the fire didn't mean that he was cold. All of them had been cold so often that they did this whenever they entered a room. It was almost a tic – something one did automatically on seeing a stove. Or it was like pulling up a chair.

"Hello, Tommy. Working hard?"

"As usual! I can't interrogate the same wretched prisoner a dozen times. And I've inspected the .155. What else is there to do?"

"Two more .155's came in just a few minutes ago." He looked down at Colvin. "I suppose you'll be going home now?"

He nodded. "I want to see my wife."

"Do you?" It was a curiously mocking tone. But Jantal's voice was always suspicious or ironic.

"Of course."

Jantal pulled up a chair and rocked it, with his feet against the stove. It was almost dark in the room.

"I'm staying," he said quietly. "I've just seen Ruc. They're going to use me on a psychological warfare team. We'll talk to the Jerries in German, over a loud-speaker truck. And write leaflets to shoot at them. It seems there's an American coming down to show us the ropes."

Colvin rolled himself a cigarette and licked the paper thoughtfully.

"I don't know how it'll work here. The maquis was a little rough with prisoners, after all. They can't forget that, even though they know we haven't killed any here. They're afraid to surrender."

"That's just the point. We'll explain to them they're up against the regular French Army and protected by the Geneva convention. We have a safe-conduct pass, a Passierschein, and it's signed by just about everybody of any importance. We'll shoot it over by artillery."

Colvin took his feet away from the stove. The soles of his shoes were smoking, but his back was cold.

"I'm glad it worked out," he said. "You wanted to stay."

"Yes. But I won't be here. I'll be at G.H.Q. in Sognac. I'm keeping Jean with me to drive the public address truck."

"Jean Ruyader? Why Jean?"

"I talked it over with Ruc. We can't let Jean go into a regular army unit with officers who don't know him. He's finished. *Caput.* He's had too many bullets in his stomach. You know he's so sloppy and undisciplined, in the army sense, he'd be in the guardhouse within a week. It's impossible to get him to shave. And he gets drunk on two *digestifs.*"

"What does Jean think about it?"

"He doesn't know yet. But he won't mind. You're his particular favorite, Tommy. But I think I come next."

Colvin smiled.

"Jean's my particular favorite, rather. But he certainly isn't cut out for the regular army. He's the original and complete maquisard." He relit his cigarette. It was the great defect of rolled cigarettes: they were always going out. "It's thinking about his wife that gets him down. He just doesn't give a damn."

"I know. I think if he got to see his children, he might pull himself together. He ought to get married. He's almost the only person I'd say that of. My wife tried to get him interested in three or four girls when we had the week-end in Angoulême. Each time he got drunk and insulted them. I never heard anyone so foul-mouthed."

"He certainly takes a lot of looking after."

"I know. That's one reason I picked him for my driver. He needs you, Tommy. Or he needs me. Either one of us can probably keep him out of jail."

The cigarette had gone out again. Colvin sighed, and emptied the remaining tobacco into his pouch.

"It'll be nice for you, being with your wife."

Jantal shifted his chair uneasily.

"Yes."

"I'm getting awfully anxious to see mine."

Jantal opened his mouth to say something, and thought better of it. He got up and went over to the situation map pinned on the wall. But it was much too dark to see anything. His voice came out of that dark:

"You know, Tommy? Five years is a very long time to be away from your wife. Five and a half, to be exact. It's terrible to be alone. But you get used to it, like anything else. I'm never at ease with Juju now. She gets on my nerves." He turned around frankly, and in the failing light his face twisted sharply. "Women are so damned watchful. They never miss a trick. They count the number of drinks you take, the number of cigarettes you smoke. They're always worried about you. But they're never frank. They won't say these things out."

Jantal came back to the stove; he looked down coldly.

"They'll never understand what we went through," he went on. "Even you, Tommy, you'll never understand. You can risk your neck a hundred times, but you'll never know what it's like to be a prisoner. To be absolutely powerless — And you Americans give them chocolate, meat, cigarettes. Even toilet paper! My God."

"It comes in the K-ration boxes. Along with the chocolate. Let's don't quarrel over a little toilet paper."

Jantal smiled. "All right. But do you know what Juju said the other day? She'd met a German officer as distinguished as any Frenchman she knew. She said that to me — who'd been locked up for fifty months! And what was she doing, anyway, talking to a German officer?"

Colvin stood up and straightened his tie. He didn't want to hear any more. "I suppose you couldn't avoid running into one or two of them, during the whole occupation. There are all sorts of ways it might have happened. But look — it's almost time for dinner. And it seems nearly everyone's been called in for dinner tonight. Probably something special. So let's go on in and have a couple of Pinods."

Colonel Ruc arrived late for dinner and had to pay the usual ten-franc fine. The right to levy five- or ten-franc "amendes" for every conceivable offense was one of the few Army traditions that the Brigade's mess had adopted. If you said one of the proscribed words, such as *allemands,* instead of *boches, fridolins, haricots verts,* or *schleus,* an *adjudant* called out the fine, and you had to throw the five- or ten-franc note on to a pile in the middle of the table. Otherwise the mess was as unconventional as it could have been. Officers, non-coms, and enlisted men ate together at long tables put end-to-end to form a horseshoe. And it was perhaps the only mess in the French Army where the men began dinner before their colonel if the colonel happened to be late. He was late tonight because he had spent the entire day making recommendations for the assignment of the men. He had wholly lost track of the time.

The three tables were set up in the kitchen, which opened out on to the front hall: it was the only room in the rambling farmhouse hotel large enough to accommodate the seventy men attached to the Regimental C.P. The horseshoe made by the tables was closed by an enormous stone fireplace which filled most of one kitchen wall. Large copper pots hung over the roaring fire and sizzled there, heating water for coffee and an after-dinner grog. The fire shone on the polished tile floor and on the faces of the men; and around the four walls, gleaming fitfully in the half-darkness, were more copper plates and brown earthenware jars: some of them empty, some of them filled with a rich *pâté de campagne* of pork sausage and goose liver. There were bottles on the tables, a bottle of ordinary white Charente wine for every three men, and also dozens of bottles of cognac on the plain wooden shelves behind the impromptu bar. On the floor next to the bar were the last three cases of the champagne they had found in the cellar of Gestapo headquarters in Angoulême. The champagne in itself showed that this was a special occasion.

And it was evident enough on the faces of the men. Colonel Ruc looked from one face to another. He remembered having seen that expression only once before: the first night they had eaten together undisturbed, after four days and nights of hit-and-run fighting with a Panzergrenadier regiment sent into the hills to wipe them out. There was the same blend of elation and fatigue on every face; a brittle excited tension drawn tightly over the face of collapse. Before the evening was out most of them would be very drunk. They would keep on drinking to hold on to the elation, but in the end their very sense of relief would smother them. They would give in to it finally; relax, and be drunk.

They were all of them, and not just this evening, on the brink of a greater collapse. He tried not to think of this during dinner. But he was frankly worried about his men. So long as the Brigade held together — each man knowing and allowing for the limitations of the next: that he was a slow thinker or could no longer run, for instance — he could count on it to do its assigned job. Confidence, knowing exactly each point of weakness as well as strength, had been the source of their power. But now he had the ungrateful task of sending them individually into the regular army, a specific recommendation for each. And looked at in this way, as individuals, they were not prepared. Rather, too many years of working in small teams — setting fire to farms, blowing up bridges, derailing trains — had prepared them for nothing else. Take his own case. What did he know, that a regular army colonel should know? He could hold these seventy men together, or the several thousand scattered in similar farms over the entire irregular front. But he had no idea what to do at a formal retreat or review ceremony. And he had certainly forgotten the Articles of War.

He stared down at his heaping plate of food. Perhaps he should have prepared them for this day, even in the maquis. They would have to learn everything from the beginning: how to salute properly, the manual of arms, how to make a bed. But they were too old and too tired to learn. They had been through too many years of war. He looked at the four Spaniards eating near the foot of the second table. First, four years of war in Spain, where each of them had been wounded at least twice. Then, months of half-starvation and exposure as they worked their way into France, where they were quickly put into a concentration camp. The captain in charge of this camp had become almost a millionaire, selling on the black market food designed for these refugees—and the refugees themselves had all but starved. Later, there were nine months in the mines; here the four Spaniards were never quite sure whether they were prisoners or free. In 1939, remembering vaguely the idealistic slogans of 1934, and remembering also the German planes, they enlisted in the French Army. Three of the four were wounded again in May of 1940; and one of them, prisoner for twenty-four hours, had all his teeth knocked out when he admitted having fought in Spain. The four found their way to the Brigade's maquis early in 1943. Summarizing so from the personnel cards in his office, Colonel Ruc could see a kind of pattern in their ten years, in the lifetimes that these ten years had been. But the men themselves, stupefied, had lost all sense of pattern and time. And these were the men frightened Paris bankers expected would start a revolution! If sufficiently drunk they could remember a few bars of the *Internationale;* or, asked point-blank, they might say they were fighting for the happiness of mankind. But that was all that remained of their communism, of their original crystal resolve. Each of the four was married, and had children: they had rubbed and almost indistinguishable photographs to show. Somewhere, beyond and over the ten years of somnambulistic wandering, families awaited their return.

Where could he send such men? Or all the others: the Russians, the Czechs, the Poles? He could turn the two Germans, Hannes and Willy, over to the Freies Deutschland committee in Paris. But how could he send his four Spaniards back to Franco's Spain? And there were not a few of the Frenchmen who, after only six years, had had too much of war. Lieutenant Jantal had promised to take care of Jean Ruyader, one of the original seven. But Jean was not the only one who—wounded repeatedly, with family lost or killed—drank recklessly to keep himself going, to shut out these things. Lieutenant Colvin had spoken of seeing many such men wandering the Paris streets aimlessly in the last days of August, terrifying civilians with their patched uniforms and their unshaven faces, the knives and grenades in their belts. Even a few of his own men had joined that pitiful hegira of isolated saboteurs, desperately certain that they would find something in Paris to reward their years of work. The results, a new government that had changed everything, would stare one in the face; and there would be work for all to do. Instead they found themselves ignored or shunned as the Parisians lined the streets to cheer the passing American tanks.

Colonel Ruc shook his head and finished his glass of wine, as though to dismiss these things. The noise of the seventy men, most of them now talking at the same time, crowded in cheerfully. Captain Morel looked at him, worried: "You're not eating at all!" At the far end of the table on the right, already drunk, Jean Ruyader was singing *Je suis seul ce soir* in his husky voice of a Paris gamin. A few places nearer, his still boyish face shining, Lieutenant Colvin was explaining the difference between rugby and American football. To his left a group of sergeants were planning what they would take with them to Paris for the holiday dinners: ducks and geese, butter and cognac, jars of *pâté de campagne.* It was simply a question of how much they could get on to the train. For behind all their words and their faces was the single thought: They were going home.

And that was a great deal — how much, Colonel Ruc realized when abruptly he thought of his own apartment in Paris, as it had been before the Germans took everything away. Later in the evening, over coffee, he would have to make a speech. He would review the figures he had compiled on the Brigade's history: the number of trains derailed, the number of Germans killed and taken prisoner, the bridges and factories blown. He would particularly try to tell Lieutenant Colvin what he had meant to all of them, and wish him a good trip home. And he had planned to warn the men of what awaited them: how different and at first exasperating the regular army would be. But he didn't have the heart, now, to spoil their celebration.

Yet he would end, as he had planned, with a plea for tolerance and understanding — tolerance for all the poor ordinary civilians who had not fought during the four years, and whom they now so much despised. For they had paid the price of their virtues. After working so long in teams the men could no longer think as individuals. In the same way, having so stubbornly refused all compromise, they could allow for no weakness in others. They had come full circle, Colonel Ruc thought bitterly. They longed for a leader whom they could obey, and who would harden into law their deep contempt. The maquis, founded on a faith in the average man, threatened to become an élite. There had not been time to re-educate them; what could he do now, at the last hour, with a few words?

He would quote from General de Gaulle's Rouen speech: "France has need of all her daughters and all her sons." For this would be the hardest task that each would have to face: to readjust himself to the common fallible world; to become once more part of that world. In the three years his men had learned to kill single men silently, or to kill hundreds riding in a train. They had learned to steal food, tobacco, arms, whatever was needed to keep the Brigade alive. No doubt, in their rare hours in a town, since the liberation, they had visited each of the town's brothels. Yet they remained, in a deeper sense, innocents; they had forgotten the difficulties of ordinary life. This evening, casting over the words he had to say, Colonel Ruc thought he knew what the Mother Superior of a convent must feel on graduation day, as she takes one last look at her wholly unprepared white-robed charges before sending them out into the evil world.

Chapter II

Up to the coming of the two new divisions, the position of the Ruc Brigade was at best ambiguous. On its own small front, guarding the Orillan pocket, it had remained jealously intact. With a few token exceptions it kept the officers it had always had, and it might still have been, for all the signed agreements, a unit of the F.T.P. But at divisional headquarters in St. Bastide, ten miles behind the lines, the dominant tone was rather F.F.I. Though many of the high officers had been in the maquis, and all had fought in some way before the liberation, they were of a more professional and reserved cast. Better uniformed, they exchanged military courtesies precisely; in their offices they were very strict concerning military channels and the exact forms for reports. Still, they were men who could put their feet on a desk. One had to go as far back as regional headquarters in Sognac to discover the career officers, the true military mind. Here, where General Tourelle exerted and symbolized the regular army's final authority over these once independent bodies, everything was spick-and-span. Negro guards snapped to attention in front of their little sentry-boxes scattered through the town; there were section headquarters on every street. And every day the Paris courier brought more officers heavy with képis and gold braid — adornments no one at Rujon would have dared to wear.

The confusion of authorities and uniforms became even more pronounced with the arrival of the first officers of the Bretagne division — and the importance of the Ruc Brigade, which was about to disband, correspondingly declined. Colvin and Jantal found the officers' mess at the Hôtel de Bruxelles depressing and formalized; they left immediately after dinner. The half-dozen Americans were at a table apart, since they spoke no French. The five staff sections occupied a long table apiece. At table the distinctions in uniform stood out glaringly: the Bretagne division officers in their American field jackets, the reserve officers in their faded blouses of 1939, and the few F.F.I. and former maquisards in whatever they had managed to salvage — British battle-jackets or F.T.P. coats, perhaps, with poorly disguised trousers taken from the Darnand *milice.* An uneasy chill hung over all these tables, and the conversation returned inevitably to the gloomy subject of rank. Since there was a preponderance of reserve officers, it was natural that they should dwell on the inexperience and absence of discipline of the F.F.I., or on what an easy way the maquis had been to get major's or even colonel's *galons.* What the French Army needed was the orderly prudence and experience of the *École de Guerre.* From time to time an F.F.I. officer, slurring Maréchal Pétain, was sharply put in his place. The right to criticize remained in the family. But for the most part any flare-up was immediately smoothed over by banal courtesies.

An hour of such talk was as much as Colvin and Jantal could stand. They went at once to Chez Marcel, the little bar where Mme Jantal spent most of her time. It was a glittering frozen night. Jantal had remarked several times that Sognac was the gloomiest town in France. They walked swiftly through the somber cobble-stoned streets, past the shuttered windows and the gray uniform houses. Even the two cinemas were hidden at the back of dark courtyards; there were no lights anywhere, except in the half-dozen bars. They pushed their hands deep in their pockets as they walked.

But inside the little café it was bright and warm. The café was divided into two parts by the small bar, with its three shelves of bottles and its large clock permanently stopped at twenty minutes after five. There was also a glass door leading to the kitchen. They never closed it, but if someone brushed it in walking by, it tended to swing shut; M. Marcel had been meaning to remove it for years. The front room, with its two rows of tables against the walls, was for casual passers-by (though there were few of these, since the café was hidden at the end of an alley, deep in a maze of back streets). Or it was for regular customers who were in one way or another not *sympathiques:* a group of noisy aviators, couples who came one night a week to rent one of the upstairs rooms, or the hysterical Mme Fougères, who had offered herself to everyone who came to the café, even to M. Marcel. But behind the bar, in the large kitchen, was the hide-out of those who had been "accepted" – and standing at the bar one could look down enviously on them, seated comfortably around the long unpainted table, or warming themselves over the kitchen stove.

The Marcels, who reproached each other for fatness, between them seemed to fill the room. Mme Marcel had her own particular place, and her enormous body covered by a sack-like black dress folded over the table and chair. She was forty-two but looked sixty; she must have weighed nearly three hundred pounds. All day she was busy preparing or eating food, and her fat dexterous hands worked without rest at one of the two things. From time to time her body would seem to lose equilibrium; then she would take her breasts in her hands and lift them from one side to the other with a little frown of impatience. When she did this the whole table trembled, and she would look up angrily or playfully at the laughter she caused, according to her mood. Her chin fell away in immense rolls of fat.

M. Marcel's, on the other hand, was a controlled fatness. He was more than six feet tall, with a fine leathered sailor's face and a wild shock of gray curly hair. Almost any afternoon he was to be seen striding the streets of Sognac, bareheaded and with a fur-lined lumberjack, carrying a goose or duck under his arm. Sometimes he had at the same time a goose and a pail of oysters in his hands, a dozen long thin loaves of bread jammed under his arms. He was a heroic figure, with his faraway smile and his head held high; people on the sidewalk shuffled out of his way or turned to stare.

In the long hours after dinner — the table still littered, the whole room in a wild disorder of dirty dishes and overcoats flung anywhere — the Marcels held court. Here the habitués would remain or drop in for coffee and a cognac: Mme Périer or M. Terrevin, always suffering from some terrible ailment, his hands bandaged or his throat covered with wool. It was sometimes hard to tell whether a given person was servant or customer. The maid Thérèse always sat with them after dinner; she was a timid spinster of fifty whose hands were so often greasy that she offered her wrist, as a matter of course, whenever you tried to shake hands. Mme Jantal was there every evening, and through most of the day — a tall cheerful woman who tried to look forty, with her very blond hair and heavy makeup, but who looked much older whenever she relaxed and the hard brightness fell away from her wrinkled face. She spent much of the day at this table, playing *belote* with Marthe or Thérèse, or intently paring her nails. Her body was firm and she dressed with the summery daring of a Parisian, but her voice was the monotonous birdlike chirp of the Charentaise. She had in fact aged considerably since her husband left in 1939, perhaps because she had virtually spent the five years in this room, playing *belote* or minutely paring her nails. It was not that she lacked intelligence. But she had determined to wait here for her husband's return. It was the place to which he was bound to come at last — and so her monthly letters to the Offlag were filled with the details of dressing geese or stripping rabbits; of Mme Marcel's quarrels and M. Terrevin's ailments; or of the vast complications in the life of Marthe, the waitress. She had never taken the habit of reading.

Of Marthe, and Henri, her husband by common law, Lieutenant Jantal had pieced out the entire tragic story from his wife's meager details. Mme Jantal had scarcely mentioned Marthe until June of 1941, when—quite inexplicably—Marthe began to go out with Henri. Such a sweet girl, who could have made her own choice, to go out only with a plain-clothes policeman who was so often brutally drunk! Before 1940 Henri had been a salesman in Bordeaux and Angoulême. So he must have been a collaborationist, Jantal surmised—part of the dregs that floated to the surface, brightly opportunistic, in the fall of 1940. Often in the summer mornings Marthe came to work with the marks of the night before: with a black eye, or with her neck or bare legs bruised. Reading his wife's letters, Jantal followed Marthe's story from that initial mystery, through the moment when she began to live openly with Henri, to the explanation which Mme Jantal happened on at last, late in 1943. In 1937 Marthe's sister Suzanne had been arrested in Angoulême for submitting to an abortion and as an unlicensed *fille publique*. After three years of official surveillance she went to Bordeaux. She rehabilitated herself and married there; and there might have been no harm had Henri not met Marthe. But then, remembering Suzanne's life, he blackmailed Marthe into sleeping with him to protect her sister, and at last into becoming his common-law wife. The letters came once a month; during the month Jantal visualized the details. By the time he escaped he had so elaborated the tragedy in his own mind that he was surprised to find the real Marthe so young: a firm-bodied good-looking girl of twenty-five, large-breasted but with slim arms and legs, and still quietly cheerful rather than beaten in spirit; with her thick brown hair bobbed prettily, a very smooth naturally brown complexion, and large very brown eyes.

It was the first time Colvin had been in the café. This evening there were only three persons in the front room: Mme Fougères with Sergeant Mahmet, and a pert round-faced girl of twenty-one with a Red Cross arm-band and an F.F.I. badge on her cap. Otherwise she was not in uniform, but wore a very short checked skirt and a faded blue button-up sweater. She had the familiar German army shoes, but no stockings, though it was one of the coldest days of the year. She was sitting alone near the door, as though waiting for someone. Near the stove Mme Fougères stared challengingly across the table at Mahmet, a very dark Algérois; behind her boldness she was slim, tubercular, plaintive. Jantal shook hands with them and then led Colvin past the bar and down the three steps to the kitchen. They both saluted on entering the room — and Colvin smiled briefly, thinking he must unlearn this French Army habit before going home. He was wearing his new dress uniform, even his first lieutenant's bars, for the train ride tomorrow. In two weeks, if he caught an early plane, he would be home.

"Roger!" Mme Jantal chirped from where she sat at the end of the table. They had finished dinner; Mme Marcel was grinding a few real coffee beans to flavor the *café national.* The others were leaning back contentedly in their chairs. There was a great pile of oyster shells in the center of the table, a dozen plates piled on each other, and what was left of a large cheese. When they entered, M. Terrevin and the two servants, Marthe and Thérèse, edged away to the end of the table to make room. Roger made the rounds shaking hands; he had a disturbing habit of never saying anything until this was done. Then he bent over quickly to kiss his wife. Colvin noticed that her hands closed to tight fists.

M. Marcel was the first to see him standing in the doorway. He waved to an empty chair.

"Well, our first American! The very first to come here." He changed from French to English, smiling broadly. "How do you do, boy! What you think? Be seated, boy." His voice was higher, more tremulous, when he spoke English.

"An American!" Mme Marcel exclaimed. "I have to welcome him!" She waddled over to Colvin, holding her breasts out of habit, and kissed him on both cheeks.

"Excuse me," Jantal said. "I forgot you didn't know Tommy. This is Lieutenant Colvin. You can talk French with him."

"Lieutenant Colvin!" several of them said at once.

"You see, Jean Ruyader has talked about you so much."

"Once again!" Mme Marcel said, trying to throw her short arms around him. "I'm so fat I never walk any more. So I haven't been in to town to see the Americans. You're the first one I've seen. And you're a handsome boy too!" She turned toward Marthe, who was waiting with the others to shake hands. "Isn't he handsome, Marthe? He's as good-looking as a Frenchman! What do you think?"

"I agree," Marthe said, laughing. "He's very handsome!"

They sat down, and Marthe went to the bar and poured out eight glasses of cognac. There was a long silence as they looked him over: his face, his hands, his uniform. He had got used to this kind of prolonged friendly appraisal, and he said nothing. It was like sitting for a portrait; one had to remain perfectly still. But it would be nice to get to Paris, where Americans were not such a novelty.

"Where you come?" M. Marcel asked in his brisk clipped English. "Boston? New York? New Chicago? I be all those places, boy. Yes sir, that's my baby. Boston, San Francisco, du Pont."

Colvin laughed. He answered in French: "Du Pont's not a city. Though it might as well be."

"Yes, boy. I be there. U.S.A. 1912, 1913. I travel all over the U.S.A."

"Talk French," Mme Marcel said sharply. "Isn't the French language good enough for you? Besides, there's no telling what mischief you might be getting at – talking in English. And you, Colvin, you have a cigarette for a poor old woman seeing her first American?"

He took out his pack of *Gauloise ordinaire* and gave her one. "I'm sorry I haven't any American cigarettes."

"No American cigarettes!" She put up her fat hands as though in horror. "But you have some chewing-gum surely? And chocolate?"

He shook his head.

"No flour, no sugar?"

"Sorry, madame!"

"Then why did you come to France at all?"

They all laughed. But Mme Marcel looked at him severely: "I've been waiting to talk to my first American. There is something I want to talk to you about – your treatment of the Boche prisoners. Is it true you give them chocolate and cigarettes? And meat for breakfast?" Her face began to flush angrily. "After all they've done. And with our French children who have never tasted chocolate! It's a disgrace."

Colvin began to feel tired. He could see every turn the conversation would take. "We follow the Geneva convention. Besides, it's much simpler to pass out the boxes, even though they do have chocolate and cigarettes – "

"My nephew in Königsberg," she burst in. "Do you think he gets chocolate? Cigarettes? Do you know what he gets to eat? You ought to shoot them — all of them. That dirty race — "

"He doesn't give them chocolate," Marthe said. "He was in the maquis with Jean." She smiled at him. "You see, we know all about you."

Mme Jantal carefully selected a butt from the ash tray. "Why mistreat prisoners, anyway? They're just soldiers. And once they're captured they can't do any harm. If we shot them, our prisoners in Germany would be shot."

Jantal looked up, startled and angry.

"You don't know what you're talking about, Juju. They're not just soldiers. They're animals. They're Germans. Must you always be defending the *schleus*?"

"I'm not, Roger! But there were so many of them who didn't want to fight. They were civilians in uniform."

He drank his glass of cognac in one gulp.

"You disgust me. You speak without thought or experience."

Colvin was struck by the change that had come over Jantal since they had been with his wife. He lifted his glass and said *"A la nôtre!"* They all drank. It was very ordinary cognac. In their months on that cold front they had all become connoisseurs. He wondered how much a bottle of V.S.O.P. would cost in New York after the war. He turned to M. Marcel, the only one who had kept his innocent contented smile. "Tell me about your trip to America. How did you like it?"

"Okay, boy. Wait, I get you my picture cards." He got up from the table and went out the door next to the sink, which was piled high with dirty dishes.

Jantal looked at his watch impatiently. "Where's Jean?" he asked. "Tonight at least he might have been on time."

"He said to tell you he was going to get his furlough and travel orders."

"Are you going too, Roger?" Mme Jantal asked.

He shook his head. "Not tomorrow. Later in the week, perhaps. I have to wait for the American who's coming down to work with us. Tommy here is going up with Jean on the train tomorrow. The loudspeaker truck won't be here till New Year's, so Jean might as well have a two-week furlough."

Marthe looked at Colvin earnestly. "I'm very glad you're going up with Jean," she said. "He gets drunk so easily. And it's so important that he get to see his children. If he went by himself, I'm afraid he'd never get there."

"I know. That's why I waited to go with him."

"You'll go to the farm with him?"

"I don't know whether I can. It depends on when I can get a plane to America. But I'd like to go with him. He wants me to be there for Christmas dinner."

Mme Marcel cut herself a generous slab of cheese. "Airplane to America! You'd do much better to keep your feet on the ground. You know, I think Jean's afraid to go see his children alone. He wants someone with him."

"I'll see that he gets on the right train out of Paris," Colvin said. "I'll go with him if I possibly can. I have a feeling it'll be a Christmas dinner worth going a long way for."

"It's no wonder it seems a little strange for him," Marthe said. "Imagine! Four children — and the youngest one he's never even seen." Her large brown eyes filled with tears. "It would almost be better if the children could come here. Jean simply won't know how to talk to them, alone."

"It would be nice if you could go, Marthe," Mme Jantal said. "If Jean could take you — "

"I'd like to. But it's out of the question. I've thought so much about Jean's children, I'd really love to see them. And I could help to smooth things over, the first days. But Henri wouldn't think of letting me go."

The name of Henri—about whom so much in that house remained unspoken—silenced them all. Mme Marcel looked up at the door through which Henri himself would come later in the evening. Marthe got up and went to the bar to see whether the three customers who remained wanted anything. They were all relieved when M. Marcel returned with the postcard folders. He drew a chair up beside Colvin's and very carefully laid the postcards, twelve to a folder, on the table. He pointed to the first card, a photograph of the Singer Building, starkly red against an incredibly blue sky.

"That's where I began," he said in French, talking now to the others as well as to Colvin, but even more to himself. The cards were thin at the sides from rubbing. The creases where the cards joined had long ago broken; they had been attached neatly with adhesive tape now black with age. "I'll tell you the story of my two years in America. From the beginning to the end—"

It was a fantastic story, a fusion of bare unromantic truth and deliberate lies. Or so it must once have been. But over the thirty years the elaborate fiction had come to more than embroider the slender bare truth. The inventions, decorated by motion pictures and reading, had become the truth. Fascinated, Colvin tried at each moment to disengage the actual facts, which M. Marcel himself had almost forgotten: the year behind the counter of a small Twenty-third Street café; the dingy but no doubt cheerful room in a brownstone house somewhere in the Thirties (M. Marcel plainly confused the East River and the Hudson, and sometimes even Manhattan and Brooklyn) ; the four hundred dollars spent for a mail-order plot of ground in Florida; the single great trip to Niagara Falls. These things were probably true. The trip to Wyoming was problematical. For though M. Marcel described the Tetons in terms of the Jungfrau or Mont Blanc, his picture of a small cattle town near Cheyenne was far truer in its gray drab colors than any motion picture could have been.

But what a structure of fantasy had been built on these slim foundations! Visiting his land in Florida, "near Tampa and Indianapolis," M. Marcel had seen children of ten, brown and naked, wrestle with twenty-foot alligators or paddle in long canoes through the breaking surf. His own plot of ground – and here he switched into almost correct English – "commanded a prospectus over fertile fields" and was located in "the bestest residential district of Tampa." There was a modern railroad two hundred yards behind the house, "certain to increase the prestige and value of the property." There were schools near by, and "churches of every denomination." The phrasing was so exact, so typical, that Colvin was sure M. Marcel still had the real estate brochure; he put down the temptation to ask to see it.

It was possible that he had indeed bought an acre of swampland; it was certain he had never been to Florida. M. Marcel wondered whether, when he returned to America after the war, he would have back taxes to pay. It was also true that he had bought five shares of Urenio Diamond Mine stock, for he had the certificates to show. When he left New York in 1913 the mine was still in a state of "developments," and it had therefore been impossible to sell the shares. But what untold wealth the five fifty-dollar shares would represent after all these years! Going on from the land and the diamond mine, M. Marcel proceeded to stark dreams: the dream of having been, for six months, a cowboy, driving cattle from Wyoming to Florida; the dream of having lived for weeks with primitive Indians in Oklahoma; the dream of having seen fifty persons shoot over Niagara Falls in an enormous barrel. As he told of these things, M. Marcel would look from time to time to Colvin for confirmation; and a troubled haze would come over his limpid blue eyes. It was as though he were afraid memory had played him false, after so many years.

"And you're going back after the war?" Colvin asked.

"Of course! I want to build a house on my land. And sell my shares."

Mme Marcel, who had pretended not to be listening, looked up angrily. "You'll never go," she said. "We've been married twenty-three years – though I'm not as old as I look. I'm just fat. And for twenty years you've been planning to go back."

"This time we'll go. I've enough money saved for the trip. And we'll spend the rest of our life in the sunshine, growing oranges and distilling rum. I'm tired of these gray houses; I'm tired of the Charente. And I'm tired of drinking cognac."

"You know I won't go," she said. "I could never cross the ocean. And I don't want to die in that foreign land!"

"Who said anything about dying? But if you don't want to go, I'll go alone. You can come or not as you please. This time I really will go. A man's no man if he lets his wife become a ball and chain."

Colvin was not embarrassed, for he knew at once that this was an immemorial dispute, a play which had been acted out a thousand times. It was a kind of lovers' quarrel; in the security of their marriage, a way of making love.

He was not even surprised when the tears began to well from Mme Marcel's enormous wide-open blue eyes and run shamelessly down over her fat cheeks – nor when M. Marcel quietly took her hand and said: "You know I couldn't go without you. We'll go together – or we'll not go at all."

M. Marcel carefully folded the postcards again and laid them together in a neat pile.

The moment's silence was broken by the slamming of the front door. They heard someone bump heavily against a chair, and then they saw Jean's face – swollen and darkly unshaven – at the bar. He saluted elaborately. Jantal got up angrily and joined Marthe behind the bar. He was surprised to see that the Red Cross girl was still in the café. She was alone in the room. Mahmet must have gone up with Madame Fougères to her room.

"You're drunk again."

"Yes, lieutenant!" Jean grinned impertinently.

"Did you know we were waiting for you?"

"You should know better, lieutenant."

"Stop saying 'lieutenant.' Jean, you're incorrigible."

"Yes, sir. Marthe – two cognacs for me and my good lieutenant!"

"You've had enough to drink. Did you get your furlough and travel papers?"

"No."

Jean picked up his own glass and touched Jantal's. He drank the cognac slowly but without once lowering his glass.

"No! You mean you forgot?"

"I didn't forget," Jean said, trying to sound casual. "They won't let me go. All leaves have been canceled – for a few days, anyway."

"Are you serious?"

"Of course I'm serious. *Merde!* But what do you expect from a screwed-up, snarled army?"

Jantal called to Colvin, who got up and came to the bar. "He can't go. All leaves have been canceled. Postponed, rather."

"I wonder what that means?"

"It doesn't mean anything," Jantal said. "The clerks simply have to catch up with the paper work."

"It wasn't a very good idea," Jean said. "Home for Christmas! I must say I'm glad. What the hell would I do with four brats on my hands?"

He lolled against the bar, and for the first time he noticed the girl with the Red Cross armband. He walked over to her unsteadily. "Hello, baby! How many brats have you got?"

"More than you'd suppose, from my looks." She smiled up at him brightly.

He leaned over and stared at the F.F.I. insignia on her jaunty little cap. "You're a cute trick. But I don't like to see girls wearing things like that. Just as though they were earrings. Men died so we could wear that badge, one day, out in the open. And you stick it on to look pretty. You could be arrested for wearing that."

She refused to get angry. Colvin noticed how restless her small blue eyes were. "No I couldn't," she said. "I'm in the Morny Brigade. I was in the maquis two years."

"Where's your uniform?"

"Where's all our uniforms?" She was still faintly smiling. "Here's my F.F.I. card." She took a man's wallet out of her pocket and showed him the card. He looked from the photograph on the card to the girl's face, still frowning. Then he said in English: *"Okay!"*

"You're satisfied? I'm forgiven?" She fished in her pocket

again and brought out a small black automatic pistol. It was one of the old Spanish ones, but she had kept it very clean. "I suppose this is a kind of calling card too. I've always got it with me."

"All right, you're forgiven!" His tired face gathered into a surprisingly youthful smile. "But what are you doing out here by yourself? Why aren't you in the kitchen – with the others?"

"I was waiting for a soldier. We had a fight yesterday. I guess he isn't coming."

"If you were in a maquis you hadn't any business falling in love."

"You're crazy," she said.

"Okay!" he said again, with amusing emphasis. He took one of her hands and pulled her up from her chair. "What's your name?"

"Yvette."

"Maquis or real?"

"That's my real name."

He put his arm around her waist and led her to the kitchen. "All right, Yvette. And now come and have a drink with us. We've even got an American. He was in the maquis with us. Do you like Americans?"

She looked at Colvin, and smiled. "That depends!"

It seemed hours before they decided to go to bed. It was snug and warm in the kitchen; and outside the rising wind pounded and drove against the single window. The streets were solid with ice; it was too cold for snow. And at the end of the walk through those black streets were their unheated rooms – even the water faucets frozen, and the humidity such that the towels and the sheets on their beds would be moist and stiff. As long as the Marcels let them stay, they put off going home.

From time to time Marthe went to the radio to try to get the American soldiers' program. Whenever she tuned in a Spanish or Italian station she would ask Colvin whether the announcer was talking English. Radio Paris and the German stations were coming in very strong, but the American program faded and blared so irregularly that at last this began to get on their nerves. An orchestra on Radio Paris, playing *"C'était un jour de fête,"* got Jean started singing, and soon he was standing at the end of the table, going through his long repertory of maquis songs and Paris blues. He had a harsh, deeply emotional voice, a mocking slipshod gamin's voice deepened by pity. He got very sentimental when drunk, but the tenderness was controlled by an underlying toughness; his eyes by the fatigued droop of his mouth. Yvette joined him in these songs, whenever she could remember the words.

Later, like children petulantly boosting their school teams, they argued the virtues of their respective maquis: boasted the number of Germans killed, the number of towns captured, the number of trains derailed. They spoke of each other's leaders with that kind of fiercely expressed contempt which masks respect. In the end, reluctantly, Yvette told her own story in detail. At seventeen, in 1940, she had been a typical *jeune fille bien élevée,* living on the Avenue de la Grande Armée and going out in the evenings only in the company of her parents. But three summers later — restless, aware of the barrenness of her life — she ran away from home and in due time made her way to the Morny maquis in the Haute-Vienne. She recognized now that her motives had been mixed: she had gone more for excitement than to serve a cause she little understood. Her mind had been full of *carbonari,* of *Fra Dia-*

volo and Alexandre Dumas. But the hard unromantic life of near starvation, which almost sent her home in the first week, at last taught her why she and others were there: the endless hours of training with the little equipment they had, the nights sleeping in dirty barns; or the mutilated body and face of a man for whom she had cooked breakfast that morning; and, more and more frequently, the quaintly coded messages from B.B.C., which told them they were not alone. Two months after she joined the maquis the first American agent was dropped by parachute. The parachute caught on a tree, turning him over, and his back was broken by the fall. He died the next day as she watched by his side. After that she never thought of leaving the maquis.

As she told it now, the strength of others had in this way repeatedly come to bolster her own weakness. In October 1943 she began the perilous liaison work between the maquis, Paris, and Bordeaux. On her first trip to Paris she learned that her parents, though they would not betray her, would never receive her again; the father was a director of the Banque de France. In November she was arrested near Libourne and imprisoned by the Gestapo in Bordeaux. She had been identified on the Angoulême train by a former schoolmate. She remained in this prison for three months.

The Gestapo, far from convinced of her guilt, submitted her to a half-hour's torture each day. On these occasions she was stripped to the waist and whipped with a small cat-o'-nine-tails; three strokes followed invariably by ten minutes of questioning and then the cat-o'-nine-tails again. But what she particularly remembered was the little glassed-in observation room from which Gestapo officers and visitors, French *miliciens* no doubt, could watch the torture. Ashamed of her naked breasts, she tried not to look at those smiling or cold faces pressed against the glass. The humiliation and the pain, small enough each day, yet began to accumulate; and she declared that she would have given up at last and told what she knew, had it not been for the courage of one Parisette, a seventeen-year-old girl who shared her cell. There was no question in the officers' minds about this girl: she had valuable information. She was made to sit naked on a hot stove. After two days there was no longer any flesh, but the torture was continued until at last she died of infection and pain. Each night, thrown back into the dark cell, she repeated to Yvette desperately, as though this were a talisman against death as well as treason: *"Soyez une bonne française."* In the end, to her surprise, Yvette was released; and after a month of cautious detours she found her way back to the maquis.

The story itself was not new, Colvin reflected. It was almost commonplace, because such things had happened throughout France over the long years. And the seventeen-year-old girl who died was not the only one to have been carried through such an ordeal by a quaintly antique phrase that would have been banal or cheap in another context or a more peaceful life. What astonished him rather was that Yvette remained so girlish in appearance; so unmistakably twenty-one. It did not take him half an hour to know that she would become, if he wanted, his mistress; that she was almost unbearably deprived of love. Talking to Jean, she carried easily the maquis profanity and slang; she gave better than she took. When she talked to the others the hardness fell away completely, and only an occasional word betrayed that she was no longer the girl who four years before had lived her quiet shuttered life on the Avenue de la Grande Armée. The screwed-up mocking laugh and the girlish smile replaced each other effortlessly. There was no moment of transition between the two.

But later in the evening Colvin was to see another expression on her face: a mingled expression of bewilderment and shock. He saw it when, shortly before midnight, Henri came to take home Marthe. She saw him for only a moment: a thin handsome face behind the bar, half hidden by the high turned-up collar of his overcoat; a man of twenty-five. "Are you ready, Marthe?" That was all he had said — and Marthe had put on her coat in almost panic haste. Then they were gone; she had not even said good night. But Yvette continued to stare at the place where Henri had stood.

"Who was that?" Her voice was almost frightened.

"That's Marthe's husband," Jean said. "One of these days I'm going to kill him."

She looked at him uncomprehendingly. "I mean, what's his name?"

"Henri Peytrou. He's a cop."

"Yes," she said. "Of course. You couldn't mistake that. But is he from Sognac?"

M. Marcel looked at her queerly. "He came here in 1940. He worked for the Police Spéciale here in town."

"It may be that he's just a type," Yvette said. "But I swear I've seen him somewhere. Even that I've run into him one way or another. Was he away from Sognac ever?"

M. Marcel shrugged his shoulders. "You know the Police Spéciale. They're always disappearing for a few days. Even Marthe didn't know where he went."

She took a cigarette from her pocket and lit it. She

studied the burning tip intently. Then she tried to smile. "I guess it's just my imagination. I'll always spot policemen. And I'll be afraid of them for the rest of my life."

Colvin got up and turned on the radio. "In any case, he was a pretty gloomy apparition. Let's see if we can't get some music to cheer us up."

But it was twelve o'clock, and nearly every station was giving the news. There seemed to be a peculiar urgency in the voices of all the announcers; for once, they had dropped their tone of bright optimism. And with no small reason. This was the midnight of the 18th–19th December: the first disturbing reports had been confirmed. Taking the initiative of surprise, von Rundstedt's small thrust in the Ardennes had swollen from regiment to division strength, from division to corps and army. In fact, the American troops must have been taken completely by surprise. They were definitely falling back.

Chapter III

For Jean Ruyader, a day in which he was left alone with his thoughts was a bad day. In the maquis or on the Orillan front he was always with others. In the dark mornings he awoke to the sound of breathing beside him, and the shack or dugout might be warmed by the breath of a hundred men. Or alone on a mission or reconnaissance patrol, he was alone with the enemy — and this was a kind of companionship with his own concentrated attention, his tight nerves. But here at Sognac he went to bed as late as possible, to put off the cold and the first sleepless hour alone. And in the mornings, unless Lieutenant Jantal wanted the car, he slept as late as he could. It was one of the bad things about being an *adjudant-chef* in the regular army: he had a room of his own.

This morning he awoke for the first time, by habit, at six o'clock. Pulling the covers over his head, he managed to go back to sleep at once. He awoke again shortly after eight, desperately thirsty. The sheets — the first he had slept between in four years — were damp, stiff, and cold. A chilled gray twilight framed the steel-shuttered window, falling on his heap of clothes on the floor. But the rest of the room was dark. If he got up for a glass of water, he would be completely awake. But if he didn't take a drink, he would lie sleepless and shivering for hours. He threw back the covers quickly and went over to the basin and took a long drink from the pitcher of icy water; then he turned on the light and put his trousers and shirt on over the underwear in which he had slept. The socks were stiff from dirt as well as cold, but he would save his clean things to wear with the new uniform, for the Christmas trip. There was something comfortable about the grease stains on his mackinaw, and the pockets curved out to fit the bulge of his fists.

He was trying to decide whether to wash his face in that cold water when it started for the first time that morning: the sense of empty tubes or sockets in his stomach, where the bullets had been; and at the same time the dull cold ache above his knee worked upward until his whole body was shivering. He limped over to the table — a woman's vanity from which he had angrily swept all the gewgaws — and poured himself a glass of cognac. Then he tried to light a cigarette. As he snapped the damp lighter helplessly he felt the cognac go down and down until it filled those empty places. He could see the tubes and sockets as clearly as he could see the empty glass; and in an image that crossed the dark he saw also the bright flare of a bullet fired at a hundred yards. Four bullets — four empty places that had to be kept filled. But also, with no cigarette, his stomach was folding over itself and tying in loose knots. He found a match in his pocket and struck it against a matchbox shred. And he closed his eyes to wait for the sickness to come. It would last for a minute only. Then he would be warm.

He went downstairs on tiptoe. M. and Mme Deschamps were arguing good-naturedly behind the door to the dining-room; no doubt they had built a fire, and the child and the dog would be huddled before it, to remain there all day. For a moment he considered going in and asking for a cup of coffee. Instead, he went to the backyard and urinated on to the snow. The snow was melting after a night of hard rain. It was a gray closed day, and still too early to tell whether the wet ground would freeze over again. Above that low ceiling a single plane throbbed irregularly: it was either the German courier plane for Orillan or one of the Junkers captured by the F.F.I. He was suddenly and sharply angry to think that the pocketed Germans were still getting whatever they needed: mail by the courier, food by boat from Spain. A submarine had even brought a load of oranges from Spain. And why didn't de Gaulle, knowing this, declare war on the Spanish? Jean spat into the snow.

Out on the street, people were hurrying to work, but hurrying chiefly because of the cold. A man kissed his wife in the doorway of the house next door. The woman was wearing a loose blue house coat, and she was smiling quietly — the way Marthe smiled at him from beneath her heavy brown curls. What he envied the man was not this brief kiss, but the fact that the woman would be standing there at noon, waiting for him to come for dinner; and waiting again at the end of his day. Behind each closed door, behind each window there was warmth — and why hadn't he the right, after his four years of barns and open fields, to go into any of these houses and take what he wanted? Yet he hadn't dared ask Mme Deschamps for a cup of coffee. Ahead of him on the street, a "naphthalene," a 1939 reserve officer, was walking gingerly, picking out the dry spots; he had an immaculate brown leather brief-case under his arm. And on the other side of the street three shopgirls with white knee-length stockings were almost running against the sharp wind. It was as though they were running away from him.

All collaborators: let them run! There were times, coming out of the cinema, for instance, when seeing so many girls at once made him almost sick — sick with disgust because, though dressed as Parisian girls of twelve would dress, with their white stockings, they had nearly all slept with the Germans. Sognac was said to have been the most collaborationist town in France. He could well believe it, looking into those hostile, sullen, secret faces. The whole life of the town was guilty, clandestine. You only caught glimpses of it: a fire through a half-opened window, a face at a door. You saw no one but soldiers and brandy dealers in the cafés and bars. Some even now would not admit their mistake. One of the town girls had managed to work her way up to the front and had then crossed the lines by dark to join her German Feldwebel in Orillan. It was where they all belonged.

He realized suddenly that he had walked a quarter of a mile without feeling the pain in his leg: he had limped by habit. Passing a bakery, he considered going in and asking to buy a loaf of bread. The woman would not even smile; she would merely point casually to the posted sign forbidding the sale of bread to soldiers. And who was she to refuse him — she who had sold bread to the German soldiers for four years? He limped on angrily, feeling again the need for a glass of cognac, but this time to quiet his nerves. He went into the *Coq d'Or* and ordered the cognac and a glass of coffee; the waiter walked away without saying anything. He went over to the stove to warm his hands, and felt again the emptiness of the tubes where the bullets had been. The wall behind the bar was hung with shiny copper pots; the owner of the bar must have been a collaborator too, to have been allowed to keep them.

And then abruptly he was no longer angry, but tired and a little sick. The anger had simply fallen away — and it was as though a hard firm support had collapsed inside him. He went to the toilet and washed his face: the two-day beard was uneven and scrubby under his fingers, caked with dirt. It would cost only five francs to have a shave before going over to see Marthe at Marcel's. She would be surprised to see him clean-shaved so early in the day. But what he really needed was a bath. He looked at himself in the streaked mirror. And he knew that it was neither a shave nor a bath he needed: it was ten or fifteen years of his life.

His matted black hair stuck out from under the greasy cap in two thick blobs; his shirt, where the collar had wrinkled over, was black with dirt. There are times when your mind sleeps, and in its sleep returns to a time long past. You look at yourself in the mirror, expecting to see yourself as you were then; and it is almost a stranger's face that stares back at you: tired and old, decayed. Jean was thirty-seven years old, but four years before he had looked twenty-six or -seven. Now he looked more than his age — chiefly because his face seemed to fall away from his forehead loosely, rather than build up to it. His lips were cracked from smoking and from the cold, and when he licked them his uneven teeth showed, dark brown with nicotine. He ran his hands, still dirty, over his face. And he thought: "She's dead. She can't see me." And then, aloud: "I don't give a damn."

He went back into the café and sat down. He drank the cognac quickly and sipped the coffee and lit another cigarette; and he tried to think how comfortable he was, sitting in the warm café, doing these things. But he could not think of this for the rest of the morning; the protection which he had thrown around himself was not so deep. He considered desperately reading a newspaper. But it was something he had never done. Already at nine o'clock the day stretched interminably before him. And memory, which he had held off safely for more than an hour, ineluctably and softly crushed in.

It was perhaps because he had run away from school at fifteen that he could not read a newspaper now: he was unequipped for a quiet life. It was hard for him to remember beyond that fifteenth year, so much had intervened. Yet his whole life had been shaped by war. As a child he had dogged the footsteps of the American soldiers billeted near the République, asking for chewing gum. Of his father he remembered above all a particular evening in October 1917: how, on his first leave from Verdun, he had staggered into their single attic room on the Rue du Temple and had fallen face down on the bed. The next day, while his father slept, he had unpacked the fascinating barracks bag — the mud-stained underwear, the torn socks, the caked shoes — hunting for some neatly wrapped gift for himself. Later in the week, though his father at thirty walked like an old man, the three of them wandered along the boulevards hand in hand. One night they even went as far as the street fair in Montmartre. After eight days his father returned to Verdun; and a month later he was killed. There followed months from which Jean visualized starkly his mother's face, though only at a distance of more than twenty years could he recognize her sorrow, her sickness, her fatigue. He did remember well the last week of her life, in 1919, when she contracted typhus fever and died: a victim also of the war — of poverty, hunger, and cold. "What's to become of you, Jean?" were the last words she said.

What was to become of him was ultimately associated with these facts, though the social conscience which they could have been expected to produce became coherent very late. At twelve, thrown on the resources of a fiercely Protestant uncle, he was put into the Lycée Montaigne as a pensionnaire — and of the three years there he remembered scarcely more than the bi-weekly afternoons of play in the Luxembourg, and the silent Sunday dinners of cold mutton with his bachelor uncle, under the shadows of St. Clotilde. Oh, and he remembered too the licorice-flavored sticks of wood which the other boys bought for five centimes: in the end he ran away from school simply because he was allowed no money at all. One Sunday afternoon he walked to the République; and stayed there. For two warm spring nights he slept in an alley. The third day he got a job at the slaughterhouse at La Villette. Compared with other war children, he was large for his age; he could pass for seventeen. And his job was easy enough: by means of a long pole to direct the cattle through the runways that led them to the slaughtering machines. All day he stood astride the narrow runway, disentangling horns, directing traffic. It was a lonely job

— but in the evenings he could, if he chose, go to a corner café for a few beers.

Perhaps it was because he made this first break so easily that he made so many further ones. Many persons, for want of such an early experiment, think it impossible to break thus with the past. But scarcely a year after he had left the Lycée, he was steering a barge on the Canal du Midi: carrying Pau bérets and sandals from Toulouse to Narbonne; Béziers wine and casks of Banyuls back to Toulouse. The transition from the smells and bellowing of the stockyards to the sweetly placid life of the barge was abrupt, and through all his wanderings Jean remembered his seventeen-year-old's dream of keeping a café and locks somewhere along this canal. The course of the canal and of the often parallel highway was marked by immaculate twin rows of white-barked platanes. Years later, in Indo-China, he was homesick only for those perfect regular trees.

That peaceful time ended in December, when the barge was laid up for repairs to the rudder. It would be cold in Paris, and the war years had taught him to prefer hunger to cold. Instead he went farther south to Port Vendres, where he worked as a longshoreman. He stayed there two years because he was in love with a girl in the house where he lived. The work and the sunlight strengthened him; he grew no taller, but he gained thirty-five pounds. Through the two years he watched wistfully the small tramp steamers and the P.L.M. passenger ships, easing their way out of the tiny port on to the blue Mediterranean on their way to Algiers. He unloaded great casks of oil, figs, and dates; he loaded barrels of wine. In the summer of 1925 he quarreled with the girl — whose name he had now forgotten — and went to sea. He was eighteen, good-looking, darkly tanned to the waist. And he was ready to liquidate the frustration and the outward peace of two years. He could not remember the girl's name; but he could remember still with agony her last-minute refusals, as they lay hidden in the sloping vineyards: the extraordinary whiteness of her thighs against the black earth and the rusted leaves.

The trip to Algiers became two trips around the world, and lasted three years. Now at thirty-seven, after two years in the maquis without women, he could hardly believe the exploits of the boy of eighteen, nineteen, and twenty. Memory telescoped the long drab voyages and stylized his first impressions of foreign lands. What he remembered was falling from the arms of one woman into those of another. He could look back on those passionate hours only with amusement now: on the New Orleans movie usher (a cold frightened girl of sixteen) and the daughter of an Argentine millionaire with equal amusement. On another occasion he had been with a Japanese girl on a sampan journey from Kobe to Shanghai. The trip lasted three weeks. He never had the most beautiful girl of all: a Tonkinese coolie whom he saw one hot afternoon while working for the Hongai coal mines in Indo-China.

In 1928 he returned to France, just in time for his year of military service. The years at sea, the hard conditioning of pulling ropes and lifting bales, stood him in good stead, but except during the maneuvers near Nancy he was made restless by the endless formalities of army life: the parades and retreat ceremonies, the daily cleaning of his gun and uniform. He could not stay awake through the long academic lectures; it hardly occurred to any of them that some day they might wear uniforms again. If the experience meant anything at all, it was its momentary evocation of his father, that October night of 1917, coming home on furlough from Verdun.

But such evocations were rare. He had never been a reflective boy, and at twenty-one, lazy and remembering only enough of his childhood to protect himself from drabness and discomfort, he was content to live. He was unreflective, but also handsome, experienced in an adolescent way – and with a very good rough singing voice. For two years, at twenty-two and twenty-three, he sang in cafés along the boulevards, dressed in sailor's blue, and once or twice appeared at the *Caveau de la République* and other small cabarets. The months flowed comfortably by. The even tenor of his life, immersed in daily motion pictures and endless *apéritifs,* was scarcely ruffled by a succession of brief affairs. He talked an easy brutal slang, and he had innumerable casual friends. It was a life so barren and monotonous that it was impossible for him to discern how empty it was. When he left once more to go to sea he did this not so much to escape boredom as to get away from winter rain and cold. This time also he stayed away three years.

He came back unchanged, except that he was convalescing from malaria. Indeed, anyone who watched Jean closely between his seventeenth and twenty-seventh years – there was no one to do so – would have thought it impossible for him to change. But it was not to be so. Landing in Marseilles in October of 1934, he hitchhiked up the Rhône valley, and on the second night, stranded, put up at a large farmhouse near Beaune. He asked permission to sleep in the barn, but was invited into the house – just in time for a birthday party, as it happened. And it was then that he met Anne-Marie. He first saw her emerging from the small trapdoor to the cellar with two bottles of wine in each hand. He saw her lovely dark hair and then her soft eighteen-year-old face, smudged from bumping against something in the cellar; and when she saw him her small mouth opened in surprise. She quickly rubbed her face with the back of her hand, but this only spread the smudge to her nose. This struck him at once as so funny and so appealing that he began to laugh. Embarrassed, even a little indignant, she brushed past him and ran upstairs – and, hearing her wooden-soled shoes on the stairs, he was already in love. He had meant to spend one night in the barn, but instead he spent six weeks on the farm, working with her in the kitchen and in the fields. In December they were married.

At twenty-seven his life was changed completely, and it was thanks to her that he began to grow up at last, to become aware of the world around him. Twelve years had drifted by since he left the Lycée: twelve years during which he had had ample opportunity to observe a good share of the world's suffering and injustice. But it took their love, the quiet happiness of their life together, to make something coherent out of those blurred impressions. After their marriage they moved to Paris, quite naturally to the Faubourg du Temple; he settled down to a steady job in a small paper-cutting factory. It was here that he had his first contact with workers and the labor movement, and, shortly afterward, with the Communist party. He was still unable to read a newspaper, but he began to listen to the conversation of his friends and fellow-workers. His starved intelligence was fed late but at last.

Innocent country girl that she was, Anne-Marie yet remade his life. He knew this and was grateful. But the memories which his mind refused so stubbornly were of a different kind: of small things, of the ways she looked at him and smiled. Of how, when he put his fingers behind her head, she pressed back against them until her small perfect chin touched his own. Or how in the cold mornings she rolled him over in the bed so that she could snuggle up against him, her knees crooked up into his — first pushing his shoulders gently with her fingers and then actually taking his body in her hands and rolling him over as though he were a child. There were the hundreds of ways in which she tried to surprise him — from that first Christmas morning, two weeks after their marriage, when he found one of his shoes before the fireplace, filled with gaily wrapped little packages: razor blades and pencils, *bouchées* and mints. When he came back from work he would always find her hiding behind the door — as though to tell him that she had waited all day for this moment, for this first long kiss. And there were the long evening hours when, children once again, they played at cards or horse races or roulette on the thready brown carpet, stopping now and then to wrestle or make love. It had been five long years of love-making; and he remembered, intolerably, the warmth of her body under his; the way her mouth opened to be kissed, like the mouth of a bird waiting to be fed; the tightening pressure of her fingers dug into his back; the final wild surrender in her eyes. Then he would caress her gently, and all his love would find its way into his fingers spreading her hair on the pillow.

These things deepened and changed; and with the coming of the first two children there was a new warmth between them, though abruptly his child wife had become a competent and in a sense mysterious woman. But the years with the children called to mind the fourth child he had never seen — and so inevitably the swiftness of all that followed, the memories at all cost to shut out. She cried easily; cried often out of sheer happiness, or helplessly, her eyes wide open, if he hurt her by some rough or careless word. Then how much she must have cried, have suffered how much, in the last four lonely years of her life! There had been the night he left her to spend his first night in an army barracks; or the night he left for the front—and now at last, after so many years, he could read the face of his dead mother, and the exhaustion of month after month without word. But all these things led irresistibly, skipping over the eighteen months of the war as though they had not happened, to the moment when there came a break beyond repair. That was in July 1940, and he had been back to the farm only a week before he got into a fight with a German soldier, and had to go underground. For two months he tried to get to England: once he did not have enough money to pay his passage; another time he fell upon a patriot, but the tiny fishing boat was driven on shore and wrecked. Then, until late in the summer of 1941, he helped with the smuggling into Spain. In August of that year he joined the Brigade. He saw Anne-Marie only once more, in October 1942, when he hid out for three days on the farm; he had come to say good-by before going into the maquis. And he had calculated in advance what the consequences might be—though no one can actually conceive his own death or the death of his wife. But this was the fact with which memory at last assailed him: her death. And those final tears which, if only he could visualize them, might be reconciled at last—the actual image of her face staring at the firing squad; staring through her last tears at him.

He had just finished his third glass of cognac when Yvette came into the café, shortly after ten o'clock. His mind was pleasantly blurred: it was as though she walked toward him out of the cold, into that comfortable haze.

He kicked the chair opposite away from the table, so she could sit down. She was shivering slightly, and, because she wore no lipstick, her mouth looked very soft and small. She refused the chair and sat down beside him on the leather cushion that ran the length of the wall.

"Don't you ever work?" she said.

"Not now. Don't you remember? We've been relieved. The real grown-up soldiers have taken over."

"But I thought you were to drive some kind of loud-speaker truck for Lieutenant Jantal."

"That's right. It's not many armies that use *adjudant chefs* for chauffeurs. Not so many weeks ago I was a lieutenant. If the maquis gets absorbed one more time I guess I'll be a private first class. As for the truck – it's supposed to come from England. It'll probably get here in time for the Armistice ceremonies."

She crooked her arm under his. "I can't get warm," she said. "It was too cold even to wash, this morning."

Her body was soft and yet firm against his; he noticed the whiteness of her knees, which just showed beneath the hem of her plain skirt; and the face of the nameless girl at Port Vendres flickered in and out of his mind.

"You ought to get someone to sleep with you."

She stuck out her lower lip derisively. "That's what I came here for. Imagine spending a furlough in this God-forsaken place! But we had a fight. All I've got left is the room he rented. And his toothbrush and soap. Nice American soap."

"They've got everything, the Americans. And the little Bretagne boys have got everything too. I saw one of them passing out chewing-gum the other day, just as though he was an American."

She looked up at him sympathetically. "You're pretty bitter about getting relieved, aren't you? But you've got to admit they haven't had any picnic, these last four years."

"We didn't have any picnic in the maquis, either."

"Don't tell me about it!"

"You and your maquis," he said, laughing. "But why did they send down a division? Some say it's two divisions. Why didn't they just send us the tanks and the guns? We could have finished Orillan off in a week, with a little heavy stuff. But they didn't even give us good rifles."

"We're stepchildren," she said. "The stepchildren of the war."

He didn't like the word, for it brought to mind his own four children, abandoned.

"Were you a stepchild?"

"No," she said, smiling. "But I've been disowned. You wouldn't believe it to look at me, but my parents are awfully rich. My father was a director of the Banque de France. I used to live on the Avenue de la Grande Armée."

He took his arm away from hers. "You better drink with somebody else. I lived in the Faubourg du Temple."

She frowned. "What's the matter with you today? I said I used to live there. Since then I've lived about the same places you have. Barns and ditches. Abandoned gas mains. Even in jail. Did they ever get you?"

"No. But they shot my wife."

"I know. They told me last night. And about your four children. You ought to get married again, Jean."

"Married!" he said with deep contempt. "To hell with all that."

"I mean for the children's sake."

He didn't answer. He tapped on the table to call the waiter, who was washing glasses behind the bar.

"It's none of my business, of course."

"The only person I'd think of marrying isn't free. She's

living with a cop. A God-damned Vichy cop." The waiter came over to the table. "Are you going to buy me a drink?"

She shook her head. "I'll play you for it." She looked up at the waiter. "Bring us two Pinods and the dice."

They said nothing while waiting for the drinks. Then they played silently, and he won five straight games.

"It's no use," she said. "I might as well have bought you the drinks in the first place. I never win. I guess it's because I was in the maquis — desexed, so to speak. I don't have any luck with men."

"You ought to have. You're very cute. Ten years ago I would have wanted to sleep with you."

"This isn't ten years ago. And besides I was only eleven then." She looked up at him. "Who's the girl that isn't free? That waitress at Marcel's?"

"Yes."

"Does she love her husband?"

He shuddered; the idea made him sick. "My God, no! He has a hold on her — that's all. Her sister was a prostitute. But now she's married to a business man in Bordeaux. If Marthe tried to break away, this slimy cop would spill the whole story."

She took out her package of cigarettes and gave him one. She held the lighter to her cigarette much longer than was necessary. She seemed worried about something. "I lay awake an hour last night, trying to remember. Do you know, Jean? I've seen that man somewhere. And it wasn't any place he should have been. I've got a feeling he was one of the men standing around when I was arrested at the Libourne station. But I'm not sure. Maybe he had something to do with getting me arrested?"

Jean shook his head. "Henri's a smart cookie. I don't think he'd be standing around in public, where too many people could see him. He's no fool."

"But you're sure he was a collaborator?"

"Weren't they all? The Police Spéciale, the Police Judiciaire, the Milice — what's the difference except for the names?"

"Then why — ?"

"I don't *know* anything," Jean said slowly. "Nothing for certain. That's one reason I'm glad we're going to be here in Sognac. I can look into him. And if I don't get anything on him — "

"Shh! You talk too much. Would you marry Marthe, if she were free?"

He picked up the dice and rolled them lazily. "Play for another drink?"

"All right."

This time he won three games to two. She signaled the waiter for two more Pinods. "I couldn't afford to live with you," she said. "I couldn't support you in Pinods. But I asked you if you'd marry Marthe?"

He took his arm away again. "Look at me!" His voice was much louder now, and his eyes had begun to glaze over. "Who am I fit to marry? And I tell you — I loved my wife. My God, how I loved her! The children belong to her; not to somebody else. They don't even belong to me. It's true I want Marthe, sometimes. And you can't help seeing what a fine girl she is. But I'm not good for all that any more — "

"You're wrong," she said. "You're all wrong. But I admire you for being wrong. That was the fine thing about the maquis — the loyalty. Outside the maquis there's not enough loyalty to fill your pocket with."

He looked at her admiringly: it was what he had thought so many times. "Yes," he said. "Loyalty's what you've got when you haven't got anything else."

The waiter brought the two glasses of Pinod, and they

paid for the drinks: she for the two rounds they had had together. He finished his glass quickly and stood up.

"Come around to Marcel's around twelve, and I'll give you another chance. Right now, believe it or not, I'm going to the barber and get shaved."

She laughed. "You must love her after all!"

The slush on the sidewalk had turned to hard ice, and the faces of the shoppers hurrying along were red or blue with cold. A low red sun hung palely above the squat buildings; and an outdoor thermometer at the pharmacy read two below zero centigrade. Yet he did not feel the cold now; his hands buried in his pockets, he walked slowly toward the barber shop through a benign warm haze. Inside the barber shop he felt almost hot, and he took off his mackinaw. While awaiting his turn he looked through a new copy of *Images:* it was full of pictures of General de Gaulle; of soldiers marching; of tanks and planes. He barely noticed the three other soldiers waiting: an American sergeant and two adjudants of the Bretagne division. He lit another cigarette and sat back to enjoy the luxury of waiting for a shave.

But presently he was straining to hear every word the two adjudants said. They were seated across the small room from him: one a leathery dark-faced man of thirty, the other no more than a boy. It was the younger one who was talking:

"They should have been able to take care of the *schleus* themselves. You know, there's not more than five thousand in the whole Orillan pocket. There's at least as many F.F.I.'s as there are Germans."

The other one brushed off his clean green field jacket. "What I don't understand is that they never attacked. They've had them pocketed for four months, but they haven't done a damned thing. I looked over the whole file of daily reports this morning. It's always the same. 'No change' or 'Activity confined to patrols.' "

"They haven't got much, of course. Have you seen their uniforms? There's no two F.F.I.'s dressed alike. They don't have any artillery at all, either."

The older adjudant leaned back in his chair wisely. "That's not the root of the matter. Do you know what's wrong with the F.F.I.? It lacks discipline. It's not an army. It's a random collection of men who want to fight. They don't just need guns. They need training; they need experienced cadres. I saw a colonel this morning who didn't look a day over twenty-five. He was probably a private in 1939."

"A colonel at twenty-five!"

"Of course they're not all of the same ilk. I've heard of good battalions; even good regiments. But there are others like the Duchêne battalion – a rabble led by a madman."

"What did they do?"

"The Duchêne? They're not here – they're on the La Rochelle sector. It seems that for months they wouldn't even report their effective strength. They refused to be paid by the army. They were just a band of thieves. Whenever they wanted to throw a dinner they'd go out and steal a couple of cows and some pigs. And it's no wonder they didn't need army pay. Back in August they took two hundred and forty million francs from the Langval bank. It was part of 'liberating' the town to hold up the bank."

Listening, Jean wondered what to do. Even supposing these things were true, they shouldn't be talked about in front of civilians, or of an American sergeant. But he knew the Duchêne battalion and the long campaign of lies from which it had suffered. It had been one of the strongest and best organized maquis in France; and it was attacked now only because it had the highest percentage of Communists. The slimy little *attentistes,* knowing its power, were afraid.

"They did good work," the older adjudant went on smoothly. "By and large the maquisards followed orders and did their job. For every Duchêne, there were probably a dozen good maquis. But they simply can't handle a stabilized front like the one we have here. They're good guerrillas, but they're not trained for real war. They don't know how to begin!"

Jean stood up. He wanted to go across the room and smash that smug tanned face.

"Don't they, though!" he said quietly enough. "How could we begin, when we had nothing to begin with? No tanks, no artillery, no planes."

The two adjudants looked up at him, startled. He could see, out of the corner of his eye, the distaste on the face of one of the barbers.

"I beg your pardon," the older one said. "I didn't see you. I would have been more — more considerate." He seemed genuinely embarrassed.

"To hell with being considerate," Jean shouted. "You said what you thought. And it's a lie! Everything you said about the Duchêne bunch. It isn't true. You hear all that talk just because they're commies. You guys ought to have stayed out of here."

The two adjudants looked at each other, and the older one tried not to smile.

"We're the last ones who should quarrel, my friend. We ought to quarrel with the Boches, with the collaborators, with the big boys who took their money to New York — not with each other. We couldn't have got far without each other, in August. We worked together then. Let's work together now."

He had the quiet patronizing voice of a schoolteacher calming a child. Jean could hardly hold back tears of rage.

"Look at you!" he stormed. "Your slick spotless tailored American uniform! The nearest it ever got to the ground was the front seat of a jeep. And look at me!" He put his whole hand into the large ripped hole in his mackinaw. "I'm not so pretty and spotless. I've lived two years on the ground."

In the intense silence of the room the barber's clippers went on clicking busily. Outside, there was a loud continuous rumbling sound: the sound of very heavy trucks on the cobblestoned street.

"I hope they'll give you uniforms," the younger adjudant said. "You certainly deserve them."

"Go to hell!" Jean said. "And why did you come here, anyway? If they'd just sent us some guns we could have done the job ourselves. Long ago. What do you know about war that we don't?"

The sound of the trucks in the street was very loud. The older adjudant got up and opened the glazed window and looked out. Then he turned to Jean; and there was a curious, almost pitying smile on his face.

"I'll tell you why." His voice could hardly be heard over the roar from the street. "It's because we were trained to use these things."

He pointed to the window. Jean walked over to it and looked out. Fifteen feet in front of them, and speeding down the narrow street, was a twenty-six-ton tank. The tank nearly filled the street, and he watched it swing easily around the curve to the Cathedral and disappear. But a moment later there was another tank, exactly like the first: the same helmeted head showing from the turret, the same sleek powerful black girth of the tank's steel sides, the same identifying small blue map of France. Jean looked behind the second and third tanks toward the Square, and what he saw now was an endless procession of matériel: of tanks, of jeeps, of trailers mounting heavy guns. As he watched the convoy pass he felt the anger leaving him, the tightly drawn muscles relax. But he also felt a little ashamed. Had it then amounted to so little, what they themselves had done?

He turned away from the window and walked to the door. And he was conscious of everyone in the room watching him; he felt like a child caught in a grown-up's place where he was not supposed to be. How many days could their maquis have held out against such a division as this? How many days would the Germans at Orillan hold out? He felt sick at heart. He could do without a shave.

He stopped at the Café du Châlet for a Pinod. The way he was feeling, he needed another drink before seeing Marthe—before seeing anyone at all. But he had now reached the point, which would not last very long, where each drink would change his mood. Warm and comfortable, thinking of Marthe and of going to see his children Christmas, he could watch without resentment the great tanks streaming by the window. It was too late to see about his travel orders or go for his new uniform, but he still had time to go to another barber shop for a shave. It was nearly twelve o'clock when he reached Chez Marcel.

He found Marthe in the front room alone, setting the tables for lunch. She was wearing a brown checked cotton dress and blue socks.

"Hello!" she said. "That American lieutenant was in and out a few minutes ago. He wanted to know if you'd got the furlough and travel papers. He's coming back after lunch."

"I know. We're going through the Martell factory this afternoon – have a few free drinks."

She shook her head comically. "I'll reserve a bed upstairs for the two of you. You and Lieutenant Jantal certainly needed one the last time you went through a cognac factory."

He watched her bend over the tables to lay the knives and forks. Her brown hair fell over her eyes, and she brushed it away impatiently. When she straightened up again her breasts were still large and high. For a moment he wanted her badly. He thought: she was older looking than Yvette, but just as pretty.

"You're beautiful," he said aloud.

"Why, Jean!" She turned and gave him a surprised smile.

"I mean it. But especially today." He walked over to the bar. "Have a Pinod with me."

She poured a glass for him; and over her shoulder he saw that Mme Marcel was busy at the stove. When Marthe came out from behind the bar he caught her nimbly in his arms and looked down into her large brown eyes.

"See!" he said. "I got a shave. Just to look nice for you."

Something like a hurt look came into her eyes for a moment. Then she smiled again. Each day he forgot and learned again how much at peace her smile made him feel.

"You always look nice to me, Jean."

He wanted to kiss her. Instead he turned away and picked up his glass casually – as though stopping her had been no more than a moment's playful whim.

"What shall I get my brats for Christmas? I'm going to be in Paris a day, to buy them things."

"I don't know that you'll find very much this Christmas. They say it's almost impossible to get good dolls and toys. And they're dreadfully expensive this year."

"*Money*," he said contemptuously. "I'll have all the money I want. Jantal's lending me a thousand francs. I can buy seven bottles of Three-Star cognac for a thousand. And sell them for three thousand in Paris. That'll give me two thousand for Christmas presents."

"And you? You're going to live on nothing?"

"Well, fifteen hundred francs for presents. That ought to be enough. But I don't know what to get."

"I'd get them dolls. They're not very wonderful dolls, now, with their paper hair and dresses. But children don't see those things. They don't care about them. If a child can love at all, she'll love the dirtiest rag doll."

"I want to get good ones. And toy soldiers. Haven't you seen the kids here in town? All of them play soldier."

Marthe laughed. "You forget, Jean. Your oldest child is only nine, and a girl."

He sat down at the end of one of the tables and watched her put out the salt-cellars. He had the impression she was working as slowly as possible, so she could stay with him and talk. It was almost the only time in the day when they were alone.

"I wish I could take you, Marthe. I need a woman to help me select the presents."

"I wish I could go." She looked up from her work; then she came over to him and put her hands on his shoulders. "You don't know how much I wish I could go!"

"Then come."

She shrugged her shoulders. "And Henri?"

"You've got to leave him some day. You can't be a slave all your life." The words were coming easily now, the things he had wanted to say. "You ought to leave him and marry somebody else. You've got your own life to live — not your sister's."

"And who would I marry? You?"

He looked beyond her at the row of neatly laid places. "Don't joke about that!" he said harshly. "If I were twenty-five — And if it weren't for Anne-Marie — But I'm just a professional soldier now. I warn you, Marthe. Don't ever marry a former maquisard."

She smiled again, and took away her hands. "Are they so terrible?"

"They wouldn't make good husbands. Maquisards, prisoners back from Germany, career soldiers. They've lived just with men too long. Or just with themselves. Look at Jantal. He can't get on with Juju at all. She gets on his nerves."

The door opened and closed. It was Yvette. She came over and sat down beside him. She shook hands with Marthe.

"Bring us the dice," Jean said. He looked at Yvette. "I was just saying that former maquisards would make terrible husbands. What do you think?"

She blew on the dice and rolled them. "I agree," she said. "They'd be terrible."

At the non-coms' mess there was a good deal of talk about the German offensive in the Ardennes, now in its third day. Their first reaction to the news had been one of amusement. Who could take seriously the last thrashings of a dying animal? But now, after only one evening and two morning communiqués, it was clear that this was no feeble counter-thrust, and that the Allies had been taken by surprise. The corporals and sergeants who had been only in the maquis, remembering the panic flight of whole German divisions toward Dijon, could hardly believe that this in some cases horse-drawn army could still be dangerous. But there were others who had participated in such a flight, in 1940. And they remembered the first communiqués which told, it later proved, that they had lost the war: "The situation is confused. There appear to be German units behind several forts of the Maginot line." Always the Ardennes had been the gateway to France, and now already one powerful German thrust was headed straight for Sedan. But how could you believe that, sitting in this comfortable room, with the steaming platter of roast beef on the table, and the three bottles of white Charente wine? Across the room there was a table with four American sergeants, attached to the liaison mission. It seemed very natural to have them there. The contrast with life under the occupation was so extreme that it was hard to believe the war was not already over.

Later they talked about the Christmas furloughs. Jean turned to Raoul, who worked in G-1: "I meant to drop in this morning. Have my papers come through?"

Raoul shook his head. "Nobody's. There's some kind of big meeting with the General this afternoon. I suppose it's a matter of the change-over. We've all got to be here and show the files to the new men. For the moment the order stands. No furloughs, no passes."

Jean stabbed at his plate impatiently. *"Merde!* Something always gets screwed-up on paper. I'm going to be attached here. I don't have to show 'files' to anybody. I'm going to stay." He shook his head. "That's what was good about the maquis. We didn't get buried by paper."

"It takes around fifty sheets to move one soldier," Bébé said. "And we haven't any paper for the toilets!"

"Listen," Jean said to Raoul. "Tell your paper-boy lieutenant this American's waiting for me. Tell him if those orders don't come through this afternoon I'm going to take off anyway. Colvin's on his way to America. He doesn't want to spend the winter in Sognac."

"And neither do you!"

Jean drank a glass of the weak vinegary wine. "I don't give a damn. But I'm going to the farm for Christmas if I have to walk there. I have to stop off in Paris too."

Bébé whistled. "You don't want much!"

Jean half closed his eyes and saw himself walking up to the farm, a barracks bag full of gifts over his shoulder. "I've got to go by Paris. I'm going to buy some dolls and colored blocks. And Colvin can get me all sorts of things from the American quartermaster. Chewing-gum, chocolate, cigarettes. Remember those little boxes they used to drop us, in the maquis?"

"K rations? One of them had a wonderful pork pâté and a bar of chocolate."

"And four cigarettes. And powder for bouillon. Just one of those boxes would make a good Christmas present."

Jean felt much happier now. He could see his mother-in-law trying to tear open one of the water-proofed boxes, and her pleasure when she found what was inside.

"I'm going to have a whole case of those boxes," he said. "Colvin can get them for me. My brats are going to eat chocolate till they're sick."

Denis, who had been in the last months of the other war, frowned. He was forty-five and a career soldier. One of his eyes twitched convulsively all the time. "That stuff'll cost you money. In Paris the Americans sell everything. Cigarettes for eighty francs. One of those K rations for a hundred. One driver even sold his jeep for twelve thousand."

"Listen," Jean said. "Lieutenant Colvin is a very important guy. He can get me anything I want. Besides, I'm taking some cognac up to sell. I'll have plenty of money. My kids haven't had anything at all. They've never even tasted chocolate. Well, they're going to eat chocolate till they get sick on it, now. They're going to have everything they want."

"I'm taking a goose up to Paris," Bébé said. "A big fat goose and a case of cognac."

"You know what they want in Paris? Wine. Not cognac, but good *vin ordinaire*. If I can get off for Christmas, I'm going to take some St.-Emilion."

The waitress took away the empty platter of roast beef and brought cheese and apples. They took out their pocket knives to pare the apples. Raoul called the waitress over and ordered another bottle of wine. "We ought to arrange some kind of Christmas party," he said. "Just in case none of us can get away."

"None of us! You're crazy."

Raoul looked up at him seriously. "I hope so," he said. "I hope I'm wrong. It'll be a crime if you don't get up to see your children, Jean. But there's something very strange going on. I've got a feeling there won't be any leaves at all — that none of us will get away."

Jean didn't get around to picking up his uniform that afternoon. After lunch he went over to Marcel's and had two cognacs while waiting for Colvin and Jantal. It was three o'clock before they left for the Martell factory. One of Juju's cousins worked in the shipping room. He escorted them through the factory, and it was a matter of pride for him to be able to offer them samples at every point of the tour: ordinary three-star cognac in various rooms, but also the one-star reserve for Japan; V.S.O. and V.S.O.P.; even Cordon Bleu. Sometimes there were glasses to drink from, but more often they drank from the scooped-out bottom of bottles turned upside down. They were in the factory for an hour and a half, and when they came out into the cold darkening afternoon even Jantal and Colvin were a little unsteady. Jean was very drunk. On the way back he sang at the top of his voice. He was happier than he had been all day. As soon as he got back to the café he went up to one of the tiny rooms to sleep.

But once inside the room, alone, he began to feel a little sick. The room was furnished for couples who would come without baggage to spend a few hours. There was only a washbasin and the white double bed. He held on to the foot of the bedstead with his right hand and tried to untie his shoes with his left. But the bedstead lurched sharply away from him. He staggered over to the single window to open it—and a moment later found himself lying sideways on the bed, with his head touching the wall. The single hanging bulb circled crazily, as though he had struck it. He tried to get up to turn off the light, and rolled over on the long pillow. He closed his eyes.

But with the darkness the bed began to revolve slowly, and at the same time to rock gently from side to side. It was as though his stomach and his head remained in one place, while everything else moved. But presently, he knew, he would begin to sweat; he had been through this often enough before. Then he would hold tightly to the sides of the swaying bed, and in a few minutes the sweat would turn cold and the slow churning would stop. In five minutes he would be free of the sickness; he could sleep like the dead. The change always came suddenly. One moment he was desperately sick; the next moment his whole body was cold, and he was ready for a sleep without dreams.

Or so he believed. Actually, sleep brought no relief. It seemed no more than a few seconds before he awoke, screaming at the top of his voice. In his drugged fatigue he remembered only the last images of his dream. But that was enough. He had been standing with a sub-machine gun in his hand, one of a firing squad of four men about to execute a collaborator. It was a woman; she had a handkerchief tied over her face. He pulled back the cocking-piece and put his finger on the trigger, waiting for the order to fire. His whole body was filled with hatred and disgust, for the woman had betrayed seven of their men. At the same instant the man on his left said "Fire!" and the handkerchief fell away from the woman's face. It was Anne-Marie. He heard the other guns fire; and then, a moment later, his own. The bullets struck her in the chest, and he watched in horror her perfectly unmoving face, the eyes still open and alive. Desperate, he jammed his finger on the trigger and held the barrel up, aiming for her face. He kept firing until all his cartridges were gone.

For more than an hour after that he lay terrified and sick, unable to sleep. And then at some moment which he could not remember the light went out and he found his way under the covers. This time, when he awoke, it was very dark outside. He got up quickly and went downstairs. It was nearly nine o'clock. The café was empty, but they were all in the kitchen, sitting around the table. Even Yvette was there. They stopped talking when he came into the room.

"Well," he said. "What's the secret?"

Jantal looked up at him coldly. "You'll have to stop drinking," he said. "You're killing yourself."

"I'm all right. I feel fine."

"You weren't feeling fine up there," Mme Marcel said, pointing to the ceiling. "You were screaming like an animal. Marthe went up and covered you. And turned out the light. I haven't got enough electricity to have the light going while you're asleep."

Jean went over to the stove and held out his hands. "Thank you, Marthe."

"It was nothing," she said. "I just wish you'd take care of yourself a little better."

Colvin lit a cigarette and gave Jean one. "I'm afraid we're all sinners this afternoon. Why pick on Jean? We all drank too much."

"He can't take it," Jantal said. "You shouldn't drink if your head can't stand it."

"I guess I'm the guilty one," Yvette said. "Isn't that right, Jean? I fed you innumerable Pinods for breakfast."

He tried to laugh. But his whole body seemed to fall away from him. "I couldn't get the papers. They're not giving any leaves for a few days."

There was a long silence. It was Colvin who broke it at last: "I know, Jean. They had a meeting at the General's this afternoon. There won't be any Christmas leaves — for anyone. It seems they have orders from Paris to keep everyone here."

Jean kept staring at the stove. "No leaves at all? After all, there's nothing I can do here until the truck comes."

"I know. But that's the way it is. So you see, Jean, I guess I'll have to go up to Paris without you. If I'm going to catch a plane — "

"Yes," Jean said. "Of course. You've got to go."

He wanted to get out of the room. He wanted to hide his disappointment. But even a little pride didn't seem to matter any more. Everything was gone.

Chapter IV

Everything was gone: it was almost a comfort so. For there is a certain point, beyond pain and deprivation, where hopelessness sets in; one simply ceases to care. Any one of these things was hardly to be endured: the humiliation of their replacement, the loss of the Christmas trip to see his children, the terrible living dream of Anne-Marie's death. Taken singly, they would have imposed a kind of obligation to fight back. But coming all at once as they did, in a single hour or day, they left him numb. He knew now that nothing more could happen; and this sense of having reached a kind of bottom, a finality of deprivation, set him free. He was left with no choice but to drift comfortably; to live from day to day, for whatever the day might bring. And if the day brought even some small comforts, a good motion picture or a bottle of wine, he was that much to the good. Given some larger comfort, and with so much lost, his happiness would suddenly and unreasonably soar.

Saturday morning Henri left unexpectedly for Bordeaux; he would be gone three days. As soon as he heard the news, Jean hurried over to Chez Marcel. Once again he found Marthe setting the tables for dinner. She looked so happy and so pretty in her clean white apron that he couldn't stop himself. He kissed her on both cheeks and then, taking her two hands in his, swung her around the room as though she were a ballroom dancer on the stage.

"Is it true? Is he really gone?"

She disengaged her hands gently and went back to her work.

"You make me feel very wicked. Henri rushes out and you rush in!"

"And three whole days!"

She turned to him and smiled provocatively. "So you'll run off with me? To Paris? Or perhaps New York?"

He sat down and rolled a cigarette. He was so happy for her that even thinking of his lost furlough couldn't take away the feeling of lightness; or of light, as though a window had been opened to let in the clean cold air.

"What are you going to do to celebrate, Marthe?"

"Do? Why, nothing. It'll be enough just to know he isn't coming to fetch me each night."

"But you will do something," he said gaily. "We'll go to a dance tonight. How would you like that?"

"There aren't any dances. You know dancing's been forbidden since September. They don't even have dances in Bordeaux."

"Don't worry. We'll find a little village where there's a dance. It'll be in some old barn, and maybe one accordion for music. But it'll be fun all the same." He blew a smoke ring carefully. "We'll take the whole crowd. It's just too bad Colvin's gone. But we'll take the Jantals. And René, Raoul, and Bébé. And maybe that little Red Cross girl. She's pretty lonely."

"I don't think I ought to," Marthe said. "Somebody will see us."

"Don't you like to dance? I've never even danced with you."

"I can hardly remember. I know I liked to dance before the war. But I don't even remember what it was like. I'd step all over your toes."

He laughed. "I wouldn't mind, so long as they're your

toes! So don't talk nonsense about people seeing you. What if they do? You've a right to a little fun, once in a while."

She came over again and put her hands on his shoulders. It was a frank easy gesture, very natural though he had never known another girl to do the same thing. "I'd love to go, Jean," she said. "But I think you'll have a hard time finding a dance. If you don't find one, maybe we can go to the movies in Jarlac."

"Don't worry. I'll find one."

But it was harder than he thought. At lunch he told the others; Lieutenant Jantal had already promised the car, and would even come himself. After lunch he went to the quartermaster depot and drew his new uniform, identical with the British battle dress except that the blouse buttoned up the middle. Then he telephoned the mayor in each of the small villages where they had gone on other nights. At Jarlac and Segonzac the parties had been put off until Christmas Eve; at Marignac, the schoolmaster had died and the town was in mourning. St. Vaur had nothing planned before New Year's week-end. It was from the mayor of St. Vaur, however, that he heard of the tiny village of Lautrait. The only boy of the village who had escaped to England was coming back that evening, by the Angoulême bus; a party had been arranged in his honor. Jean smiled as he put down the telephone. That would probably mean a real homecoming dance, and a good deal of local cognac, forty or fifty years old. Lautrait would be perfect.

Yet to find Lautrait at all proved something of a problem: a village so small that it did not appear even on the large Air Force maps. It took them several minutes to squeeze into the car: three in front and six in back — for Paul, a corporal in G-5, was coming too. And they were scarcely packed in when they had to get out again: in spite of René's cranking, the car wouldn't start. They pushed the car halfway down the block, sliding and slipping on the ice, before the motor caught. Then they got back in again, their legs tangled hopelessly in the dark, only to find at the first turn that the worn springs couldn't stand the weight on the left side. The whole car shuddered, and there was a sound of steel scraping steel. There was nothing to do but to build up weight on the right side of the car. So Paul sat alone on the threatened left side, while Mme Jantal sat on her husband's lap in the middle. On the right they were so carefully packed and fitted that Raoul, with Jean on his lap, held his head far back to breathe. Marthe, on Jean's knees, had to duck her head far down and put her arm around his neck. Whenever the car hit a bump or turned sharply, her face brushed softly against his; or he would feel her long soft curls against his neck. The crisp feel of his new uniform was strange. But it did not seem strange at all to have her there.

They had the impression, later, that they had crisscrossed the entire countryside east of Jarlac: it was a miracle that the car was stuck only once in the rutted roads, for the film of ice in the center sloped off into miry ditches. Whatever road they took led them to large signs pointing to Marignac; already, at eight o'clock, the villages and farms were dark. But at last, directed by a succession of surprised farmers, they left the main road and, crossing several fields, found the low stone wall which they "couldn't miss." A hundred yards farther the wall ended, and they turned into what appeared to be the littered courtyard of a large farm. All the buildings were dark except one, where thin strips of yellow light outlined the door. But even here the shutters were drawn. An old woman, almost hidden by a gray shawl, appeared out of the dark and blinked at the headlights.

"Hello, grandmother," René said. "Is this the road to Lautrait?"

"You're there now. You have Jean-Pierre with you?"

"I don't know him. We're looking for the dance."

"Dance? You mean perhaps the operetta? It's over there." She pointed to the lighted door. "You'd better hurry up!"

René turned to the back seat. "Operetta? What sort of rattrap have you got us into, Jean?"

Mme Jantal laughed, and then they were all laughing heartily. The last time they had followed leads to a country dance they had found themselves at an auction for the benefit of the village's F.F.I.'s, two soldiers at La Rochelle. Lieutenant Jantal had paid three hundred francs for a battered and mud-caked hat.

"Let's go in anyway," Yvette said. "It ought to be fun."

They opened the door and went in as quietly as possible. But everyone in the room turned around. They were in the back of an improvised theater, and perhaps a hundred and fifty people were seated on benches between them and the rough platform that evidently served as a stage. In the first two rows, and clustered on the steps leading to the platform, were the children of the village. They were fidgeting and nudging each other restlessly. A dozen of the oldest women sat on a bench that ran along the wall, directly behind the stove. Several of them, wrinkled beyond age and with identical gray shawls, had dozed off to sleep. Between the children and the old women were the adults and young people: the men in sweaters or coats and knee-high boots; the girls in rather sober party dresses and the inevitable white stockings. But there were even more girls than usual with red, white, and blue ribbons in their hair. When the nine of them came into the room, one after another, there was a long minute of silence. Then everyone began whispering at once.

A man of fifty-five or sixty, with a fine tired face, came up and shook hands with them all. Then he turned to Jantal: "You're friends of Jean-Pierre, no doubt? I'm sorry to say he hasn't arrived yet. The train from Paris must have been late."

Jantal stared back at him. It was something his wife had noticed before: how slow in answering he had become. She wondered whether all the prisoners would be that way.

"I'm afraid you're mistaken. We heard of the homecoming party, and that there would be a public dance. We offer you a thousand apologies. But we more or less invited ourselves."

A flicker of disappointment crossed the old man's face. "When I saw you come in, I hoped you had news. It would be a terrible blow for my people if he didn't come tonight. But as for you — What greater pleasure could we have than to welcome French soldiers? We haven't had very many here, and we're still waiting for our first American. How many are you? Six soldiers? I'm afraid that between you and Jean-Pierre, the heads of my poor little girls will be spinning!" As he said this, he swept the room with a courtly gesture.

"Then you are the mayor?"

"Yes, lieutenant. M. Destrelle."

"But are you sure we're not intruding?"

"Of course not. We were about to begin our operetta. The children are getting nervous and we decided not to wait for Jean-Pierre. They've been waiting for over an hour already. And in any case, I'm afraid Jean-Pierre will be spoiled for such simple entertainments, after his years in England and Africa. It's just a little group of actors from the village. They put on plays every Saturday night. As you see, the stage is rather primitive. But if you care to stay, perhaps we can dance afterward – "

"We'd be delighted," Mme Jantal said. "I'm afraid we've already held up the curtain several minutes."

The mayor smiled ruefully. "There isn't any curtain. But if you use your imagination – There are places for all of you on that bench over there."

They went over to the bench, which a moment before had been filled, and sat down. Then they heard the mayor's voice, remarkably loud: "Let the performance begin!"

A very old woman, dressed in a man's trousers and with a black skullcap, thumped on to the stage, carrying a bedside table and chair. She sat down and explained to the audience that she had put an advertisement in the Sognac paper offering to sell her car. At the word "car" there was a loud knocking at the door, which she did not seem to hear. After nearly a minute of violent knocking a heavily made-up man of twenty-five came on to the stage; he was wearing a straw hat. He too turned to the audience and explained that he had come to ask for the daughter's hand in marriage. The old codger was said to be stone-deaf, so he would have to shout. But there could be worse things than a deaf father-in-law.

All of the puns and gross indelicacies possible were extracted from the misunderstanding: the "father" talking about the car, the young man about the daughter. With the suitor's first shock – when the father said "So you've come to buy her!" – the audience howled with delight. The father was a shrewd salesman, and he was going to exact a fair price. "She" hadn't been "used" very often; not more than twice a week. She was beautiful, and needed only a new paint job. Her motor purred; you never needed a crank to get her started. She was so well-cushioned that it was a pleasure just to sit there, even when you weren't using her. The suitor would turn to the audience with loud asides: "What an indelicate old scoundrel!" or "I wouldn't have believed it!" He was about to leave the room in horror when the daughter, a very tall consumptive-looking girl with heavily blackened eyelids, arrived and cleared up the misunderstanding. Then the three actors joined hands and sang a long moral ditty on the avariciousness of fathers and the foolishness of young girls.

This was the first of three such plays. After the third, the girl came back on to the stage and sang two recent popular songs, "Bebert" and "Robert des bois," and a few old favorites such as "Prosper." She acted out "Prosper" with a high silk hat, and she was just beginning the second chorus when the door at the back of the room swung open and a little boy's voice shouted, "Here he is!"

The singer's voice trailed off. Everyone in the room stood up and turned around, and in the complete silence they heard the sound of an automobile starting off. A man and a woman of fifty, indistinguishable except for their drab and patched farmers' clothes, came inside; and then behind them, standing quite still in the doorway, a tall young officer of twenty-one. He was wearing the full battle uniform of the British parachute agent, but with the FRANCE patch on his sleeve. He was immaculate, from his high polished combat boots and perfectly creased trousers to his sleek curling black hair. He was wearing both his pistol and his knife. After a few moments he began to walk toward the benches and the people staring at him: there was something terrifying about the lithe silence of his tread. But when no one moved he stopped again: there was no expression at all on his tanned, chiseled face.

Perhaps they had expected to see the boy of seventeen who had left one night four years before, carrying their sandwiches and cakes in the trousers of his torn corduroys. Or perhaps they were startled by the cool pagan impassiveness of his eyes: the face of a man who had been trained to kill silently and well. Perhaps it was because he had gained thirty or forty pounds. But certainly they had expected nothing so grand. The children on the stage, startled, clung to each other. Even the mayor, his mouth open, could not say a word. It was finally Jantal who moved away from the others and walked up to him:

"It's a great pleasure to meet you, lieutenant. And a great honor to be present at your coming home."

They shook hands. And the few words seemed to break the spell. The mayor came forward quickly and, taking the boy's shoulders in his hands, kissed him on both cheeks.

"It's been a long time," he said. The tears were running down his lined cheeks. "We thought you were never coming home."

Then everyone was talking at once, and pushing to the back of the room. The mayor shouted "Hip hip!" and everyone screamed "Hurrah!" It was the stranger's turn to be unable to say a word. Even his own gray level eyes were filled as he watched them line up eagerly; and as he kissed each adult and child in the village, one hundred and twenty-six in all.

The evening, which had started out so inauspiciously, was a great success. Before the dance they went to the mayor's farm next door for supper. There were sixteen of them at the large dining-room table, which was used only on election days and for such occasions as this. In the center of the table there were flowers with red, white, and blue ribbons running from one bouquet to the next. Jean-Pierre's parents, seated on either side of him, said almost nothing; they seemed awed by such splendor: by the gleaming array of silver, and the three wine and brandy glasses at each place. It was not a long dinner, since the nine extra guests had not been foreseen. But they had excellent St.-Emilion with the *pâté de campagne* and the steak, and later seventy-year-old brandy with the apples and cheese. Then there was champagne, and the mayor's *adjoint,* holding his manuscript close to his eyes, read a speech of welcome. Toasts were proposed by nearly everyone — to General de Gaulle, to the Allies, to the French Army and the F.F.I.; to Jean-Pierre and Lautrait. It was almost eleven o'clock before they returned to the council-room which had served as a theater.

But no one had left, and the dance was well under way. A single accordionist played from the stage. The children sat in a solid row on the platform, still wide-eyed with wonder, their chubby legs dangling. The old women of the village remained by the stove. The accordionist gave himself no rest; he alternated the familiar country jigs with waltzes played at the same furious pace. It was as though the farmers and husky white-stockinged girls had been starved for exercise. They swung and circled and hopped wildly, crashing into each other every few seconds — only to stamp off again as though nothing had happened. Jean and Marthe tried to dance the same way, but Paul and Yvette circled quietly in the protected spot in the center of the floor. Lieutenant Jantal did not even try to dance; he went with the mayor to the little bar in the next room. Bébé and Mme Jantal gave up after a single disastrous attempt. But Raoul danced with one after another of the village girls: shy fourteen- and fifteen-year-olds who clung to him fiercely and replied to everything he said in monosyllables.

Jean-Pierre was making a noble effort to dance with them all — these tense frightened children whom he had last seen four years before, playing in the muddy farmyards. The girl to whom he had been engaged all his life had married a cousin in Marignac in 1942. He was thus at once the most romantic figure and the only young man in the village for whom a marriage had not been pretty well arranged. The girls of his own age, and even those eighteen or nineteen, were married or engaged. But how could one arrange a marriage for someone in England, at the other end of the world? The village boys, gawky seventeen-year-olds who had outgrown their clothes, watched him uneasily from the corner in which they stood huddled together, nervously rolling cigarettes. For it was from these fourteen- and fifteen-year-olds that Jean-Pierre would choose his wife. And he had only to choose.

Mme Jantal found herself next to Mlle Rivière, the village schoolmistress, a neatly dressed and still pretty woman of forty-five. "My age," she thought; and looked down at her own carmined fingernails, her high-heeled shoes. She wondered why Mlle Rivière, who had apparently written the *adjoint's* speech, had not married. And she, who had been his teacher — she too must be strangely stirred by the return of Jean-Pierre, one of her children become so glamorous and estranged. Her eyes followed him closely, almost wistfully, as he danced.

"He's quite the conquering hero, isn't he?" Mme Jantal said. "But did you notice? Some of the girls wouldn't dance with him. I wonder why?"

Mlle Rivière gave her a thin tender smile. "The poor girls will never forgive themselves, once they're home. They're simply too shy. You know, they've been talking of nothing else for days. Was he handsome? What would he be like? Many of them were still little girls in 1940. They hardly remembered him at all."

"It must give you something of a thrill too. To see a boy you watched grow up come back this way — "

"A thrill? Perhaps. But it's nothing new for me. You see, I've been the teacher in Lautrait since 1916. I was only seventeen then. I had expected to go to Angoulême for another year of schooling myself. But the old teacher died, and there was no one to take her place. So this isn't the first time I've watched soldiers come back from the war. Or not come back." She looked up frankly. "My fiancé was killed in 1918."

Mme Jantal studied her cigarette. "Was it the same in 1918 and 1919? Were they as much changed in that war as they are now? I think we're about the same age, but I remember so little. I was astounded by the change in my husband, after his fifty months in prison."

Mlle Rivière hesitated; she watched Jean-Pierre waltzing with Yvette. He seemed more at ease with her than with the younger village girls.

"One boy was very much changed. He went to Paris — and he has always remained there. We used to see him once or twice each summer. He came down to Orillan for the bathing. With his wife." She turned to Mme Jantal and smiled. "We have a very quiet life here in Lautrait. We have our Sunday operettas, as we call them, and that's very nearly all. It's quite enough — but not enough, perhaps, for the soldier who has been in danger a great deal. Or who has seen all those great cities. Paris, London — "

Mme Jantal shrugged her shoulders. "City boys change too."

"Yes. It's a question of breaking bonds. All life is a question of breaking bonds — or quietly enduring them.

Even enjoying them, perhaps. I've read enough novels to know that our life here would be considered abnormally restricted. Yet we don't feel it as restricted. We feel no bonds. Or, we feel a bond tying us to the land; but not the bond that a prisoner feels, not a bond that holds you against your will."

Mme Jantal wondered whether the woman was sincere. Or had she gone to Paris, in her heart, with the man who came down to Orillan for his summers?

"There is a peculiar bond between soldiers," Mlle Rivière went on quietly. "One could see that very clearly tonight. There is a bond between your husband and Jean-Pierre which excludes the rest of us. We are the strangers. But your husband, who had never seen Jean-Pierre, was a fellow soldier. They had shared, in a sense, the most important years of their lives. So your husband could go up and speak to him. We could not."

"But what can we do about it, we who are excluded?"

"We can wait."

"Wait?"

"Yes, we can wait for the men to find their own way back. We've waited so patiently for them to return home alive; worried so much. So we can surely wait a little longer – though we'll wait all our lives if we expect them to become children again. If Jean-Pierre should marry one of our girls here, for instance – It's very likely he'll disappear off to Bordeaux once in a while, for a few days. His wife will be very much mistaken if she protests his going. She'll suppose, of course, that he is going in order to be with other women. But it may not be that at all. It may simply be that he has to get away from her for a few days – be really alone once more."

Mme Jantal nodded. "To a woman, independence is a terrible thing."

"And perhaps it is a terrible thing – the wrong kind of independence. The independence of one who lives only in his own mind. But it seems to be one of the things that happen to a soldier. Either he becomes a docile animal, or he shudders away from such docility and takes refuge in his mind. He has to work his own way back to a point somewhere between the two."

"But their restlessness! Have you noticed how much they drink? What is it they're trying to escape? You see that adjudant over there, dancing with the girl in brown? He's nearly always drunk. His wife was shot while he was in the maquis. But I wonder if we really understand what's wrong with him; what he's trying to escape?"

Mlle Rivière watched Jean waltz by with Marthe.

"He seems very happy tonight. I don't remember his drinking much, at the supper."

"I know. He's on his good behavior today."

"But I can understand. They had to hold so much in, the maquisards. And the prisoners too. There were many times, it seems, when any kind of protest would have meant punishment – perhaps death. So they had to keep quiet; they had to watch their friends beaten, without saying a word. I am an innocent country schoolteacher. But I've read a great deal, and I've watched children for thirty years. Children can teach us a good deal about the instincts of men. Men feel guilty for having kept quiet, when so often they wanted to speak out. And they have to kill, in one way or another, that sense of guilt. If for instance Jean felt in any way responsible for his wife's death – if it were because he was in the maquis – Have you ever watched a child who you're certain has told a lie? He can be very dangerous. He is capable of anything – until he has destroyed his guilt."

The two younger actors danced in front of them; they

bowed as they passed. They danced differently from anyone else. The consumptive-looking woman kept her left hand behind her back, and her partner, leaning far forward, held it with his right hand. Ignoring the music and the methodical shuffling quickstep of the other dancers, they swept around the floor with long dramatic strides. It was almost a tango. They didn't talk as they danced, and their faces had the intense immobility of professional dancers.

Mme Jantal nodded toward them. "I'm afraid they feel the bonds, don't they?"

"I'm not sure," Mlle Rivière said. "It's natural to pity them. They make such an effort to be Bohemian. And they nearly starve! But I rather think we're wrong. They get a kind of pleasure, pretending to be actors, that no Paris actor would enjoy."

Mme Jantal saw Raoul and Jean-Pierre coming toward them across the floor. They asked them to dance. Mlle Rivière gave her a quick frightened look.

"Oh, let's do," Mme Jantal said. "It won't kill us!"

Mlle Rivière stood up and laid her pocketbook on her chair. She looked up at Jean-Pierre, who was holding out his hands. He smiled encouragingly. "When I think, mademoiselle, how many times you frightened me, back in school! And how many times I day-dreamed of dancing with you. You never knew about that, of course. But we were all in love with you!"

She put her arm over his shoulder; and she was startled by the firmness there. "You'll forgive my blunders, Jean-Pierre? It's so long since I've tried to dance — "

It was not at all, Jean thought, like dancing with a girl for the first time. Marthe, when he swung her around, seemed to become a part of his own swinging motion, and not another person, a separate body whose weight must be managed and controlled. Even in the first minutes she adapted herself easily to his whims; it was as though they had danced together for years. With Yvette, no doubt a better dancer, he had been restless and self-conscious. It had been like starting a conversation with a total stranger in the corridor of a train. But with Marthe, even stepping on each other's toes seemed the most natural thing in the world. And now, after two hours of dancing, their bodies moved together unguided, and there were times when she danced with her eyes closed. She was five feet six; this would normally have been too tall for him. But now it seemed just right. Her high very large breasts pressed softly against him, and when they talked he felt her breath against his neck and chin. It was as though their bodies guided their feet, rather than the other way around.

All evening he encouraged her to dance with the others. But each time, after a few minutes with Bébé or Raoul, she would return to him before he asked. She would thread her way through the crowd, a determined little look in her brown eyes, until she found him again, lounging against the wall. She mentioned Henri only once, and then in protest against his suggestion that she dance with Jean-Pierre; she said she didn't want to waste any of their precious little time. A "Chemin des Dames" occurred every third or fourth dance, chiefly to give the village girls a chance to invite Jean-Pierre or one of the strangers. But each time Marthe came straight to him. The first time, quite as though they were alone, she put her hands on his shoulders. Had he stepped forward at that moment she would have locked her arms around his neck and pulled him to her. But this, like everything else, would have been a guileless gesture, as natural as shaking hands.

And yet he liked to watch her dance with Bébé or Raoul; to see her brown dress and bare legs appear suddenly out of the drab crowd, her bobbing brown curls and her soft smile. She was no longer very young; she had lost that kind of youth at some moment before he had met her, during the four years or more without dancing, the three years of dreading Henri. But some of this loss she had suffered in common with a whole generation slightly younger than her own: with girls who only now, at twenty-one and twenty-two, were learning to dance. They had missed something which was the right of girls of his own time: a few years of thoughtless happiness between childhood and marriage.

He thought: Even Anne-Marie — Even Anne-Marie had missed that brief hour. Until their marriage she had lived a shut-in life on the farm; and then abruptly had found herself a woman with responsibilities and obligations, soon to have a child. But he could not honestly regret having taken her away so young, and he remembered with an uprush of happiness their first days in Paris, and the way she clung timidly to his arm as they walked along the crowded boulevards. A particular memory awoke so sharply that for its brief duration he was watching the dancers without seeing them: how, as they stood in line for balcony seats at the Paramount, she had put her arms around him so gently that he noticed nothing until suddenly she gave him a big squeeze. This little thing had set them apart from the rest of the crowd; and in the dark theater he had kissed her over and over again. They were like lovers finding each other for the first time.

Strangely, it didn't hurt him tonight to think of these things. Without forgetting that his wife was dead, it was rather the happier moments of those first years that crowded in. For there were so many times in Paris when he had watched for the happiness in her face, just as he was watching Marthe's face now — the time at the Jardin des Plantes, for instance, when she had seen her first giraffe; or when, seeing two ouistitis curled sleeping together, she had smiled up at him coyly, reminded of themselves. And she had had more happiness in those few years, perhaps, than Marthe in her whole life; tonight at least neither her long suffering nor the firing squad at last could cancel out those years. He knew, without having to think about it, that Anne-Marie would have wanted him to take Marthe to the dance.

For through much of the evening she was just that: a child whose happiness he could watch. Had Bébé or Raoul leaned forward to kiss her, he would have been glad. Carefree kisses too were the right of a pretty girl. But as the evening passed, this feeling slowly changed. It was not that he began to feel jealous. Rather he was uneasy without her, as though some part of himself had broken away to dance with another — the feeling he remembered when, after a night together, Anne-Marie got up and left the room. He began to wait impatiently for the end of each dance, when she would come hurrying to him. He would light a cigarette; he would try to greet her casually, as though her coming back meant nothing at all. But, so natural was it to be with her again, he could only speak the truth: "I missed you!" he said, almost breathlessly, and as though surprised.

"And I missed you! Please, Jean, I just want to dance with you after this. Every single dance."

It was hard not to take her in his arms.

When they got back to Sognac it was almost dawn. They got out of the car before reaching the center of town, since the guards on the Place François Ier would be almost certain to stop and question a car returning at that hour, and with so many passengers. In the dark street Jean and Marthe said good night to the others and turned into the Rue du Nord without thinking to conceal that they were staying together. They had not discussed whether she should come to his room; they had not even thought about it. But when the moment came she followed him as naturally and unquestioningly as if he were leading her on to the dance-floor. It was only when they were quite alone, listening to the ice crunching beneath their feet, that Jean realized what had happened. He had come up this street so often alone, in the dark morning cold, that the sound of her feet added to his own limping steps startled him, and for a moment she seemed a stranger once more. Then he remembered that throughout the long evening and the dancing his leg had not hurt him at all.

But up in his room, when he could see her in the shaded light of the bedside lamp, it was again natural to have her there. With any other girl he would have been shamed by the barren disorder of his room, by the fact that there was no chair. They sat together on the edge of the bed like children, simply resting after the walk, dangling their legs. And then, abruptly, they felt the intense cold. The white bed-cover was damp under their hands; they watched their breath curl in the still air. She was shivering slightly, and little goose-pimples had appeared on her chest and her white knees. He took her hands and rubbed them briskly.

"Do you want a drink of cognac? It's the only kind of heating I have."

"That would be nice."

He went over to the table and poured cognac into the streaked dirty glass. "It's all I've got. Just one glass."

She sipped a little and then gave him the glass.

"Listen, Jean. Is this a requisitioned room?"

"Naturally. Why?"

"You should tell them to get a *bon* for coal from the Mayor's office. Anyone who has a soldier has a right to some coal. You shouldn't have to sleep in an icebox like this."

"I didn't know. But I don't think anything would ever take the chill off the room. It's too far gone. And if there's any coal to spare, I don't need it."

"You ought to," she said. "You don't take care of yourself. One day you'll wake up with pneumonia."

He lit a cigarette and untied his shoes. "The hard part's getting dressed and undressed. Once you're in bed it's all right, after a few minutes. Though the bed's like ice at first." He kissed her nose playfully. "Suppose you get in first and warm it up for me?"

She laughed. "But I was waiting for you to warm it for me!"

"Please — just this once."

"All right," she said. "But tomorrow night it's your turn."

"Tomorrow night," he thought; and his happiness darkened for a brief instant, like the momentary winking out of a light that at once comes on again. There might be no tomorrow night; and this one night, so inevitable, was perhaps merely cut out of time stretching endlessly behind and ahead.

Then he was watching with amusement as Marthe tugged at the slip in which her head was caught; he reached over to the bedside table and turned out the light. He went over to the other side of the bed and undressed quickly, his cold fingers fumbling at the stiff unfamiliar buttons of his new uniform. He got into bed, shivering, and took her in his arms. They held each other tightly against the cold, and she burrowed her face under his shoulder. Her breath was quick and warm. For a long time they said nothing; and he felt the heat from her body creeping over him, like a blanket of warm air. Then he heard her whisper: "Darling?"

"Yes."

"Tell me, do you always leave your clothes like that? Just a heap on the floor?"

He laughed and, turning on his back, put his arm around her; he felt her large breasts against his ribs, the soft rounded breasts and the tiny hard nipples.

"Always," he said. "I'm thirty-seven. I'm much too old to learn good habits."

He had only to turn his head slightly to kiss her forehead. Then he ran his lips softly over her eyelids, tracing them in the dark.

"You're so gentle, Jean," she said. "And do you know, some people think you're tough?"

"But I am! Do you want me to show you?"

She worked her left arm over his body and, taking his hand in hers, placed it on her breast. He could feel the beating of her heart.

"I want you just as you are."

He pulled the sheet over their heads, and the warmth drew them together. Then he began to caress her, finding her body in the dark: her cold toes and her soft curled knees. But it was, strangely, like relearning a body he had always known. And then, thinking of how much gentleness she had been deprived, he pitied her; tears came to his eyes. He did not have to tell her that he would not make love to her — for he wanted nothing in the way of later self-accusation to spoil this night. And she: it was not that she had lacked. He ran his hands and mouth over her body, and all the intense pity which he felt worked its way into his fingers. He thought of all the loneliness there was in the world; the millions deprived of love. Anne-Marie at least had enjoyed a few years during which they had completed themselves in each other. He buried his mouth in Marthe's neck and then took her face in his hands. Once again, the tears started to come.

But presently this feeling also changed. She put her hands back of his head, and held him a few inches above her. It was as though, in spite of the darkness, she were looking into his eyes.

"Are your eyes open?" he asked. He put a finger against one of her eyes, and the lashes fluttered.

"Yes, darling. They're open."

"Why? It's too dark to see anything."

"I can see you," she said. "At least, if I keep looking I can."

"What do you want to see?"

"Nothing. Just you."

That was all. It was as much as they had talked all evening. He did not at once kiss her; he did not even need to hold her tight. But at some moment during that meaningless little conversation his feelings had changed completely, from pity to love.

Chapter V

Lieutenant Colvin heard the whistle of the train with feelings that bordered on panic. There were more than a hundred persons on the long curving platform. They had begun to pick up their bags and packages, but some still clapped their hands and hopped up and down to shut out the cold of the dismal winter dawn. It was still snowing; fine powder drifted down from the skeletal roof of the station. The glass had long since been shattered by repeated bombings of the freight yards near by. And what if the train — which was the only one connecting Marseilles and Paris — had been picking up such Christmas crowds as this one all night? Perhaps they wouldn't be able to get on at all. He thought of the nightmarish ride from the farm, with no fewer than fifteen people sitting on the roof of the bus. Thank God the maid had been willing to come this far! Two hundred yards down the track he saw the engine emerge from clouds of white steam — and he looked at the maid and the four children, standing hand in hand, with the despair of an abandoned man. Tomorrow night he could turn them over to Marthe and Mme Marcel, but for the next forty hours they were his own little problem.

But it wouldn't do to let the maid know he was worried. He took out two one-hundred-franc bills and handed them to her. Throwing his barracks bag over his shoulder — he was glad now he had borrowed one, rather than depend on his officer's bag — he picked up the youngest child, eighteen-month-old Milou. He was closely wrapped in an outgrown white fur snowsuit; the hood covered everything but his blue eyes and his shapeless red little nose. He tried to settle the child in the crook of his arm.

"And now," he said, looking at the other three children in turn. "What are you three going to do?"

The oldest, nine-year-old Denise, clutched Jean's and Robert's hands tighter still. Jean was seven and Robert not quite four. "We're going to hold hands and not let go!" She repeated the words gravely and with determination, for they had gone over the problem of getting on the train at least twenty times. It remained to be seen whether they could hold hands and still manage the high steps of the train.

"Don't worry, monsieur," the maid said. "I'll see that they get on the train."

Colvin tried to look at ease. But he had to shout against the roar of the train storming by. It was the longest passenger train he had ever seen. At least eighteen third-class cars passed before it stopped; and he saw at once that the travelers were packed so tight in the corridors that their backs and faces were forced against the windows. Well, it was too late to turn back now. Forgetting all his well-made plans, he handed Milou to the conductor standing in the door of a first-class carriage and lifted each of the other children on to the first high step. He stayed on the platform, expecting them to tumble back into his arms. But instead they at once joined hands.

Luckily the conductor had gone through the car only five minutes before, and the persons with second- and third-class tickets had picked up bag and baggage and squeezed ahead of him into the third-class cars. Where there had been perhaps a hundred persons in the narrow corridor, there were only thirty or forty now. But human beings were not, as it happened, the main problem. "Chickie!" Colvin heard Robert say in his bright voice of discovery, and looked down to see that the child had put his free hand around the long blue neck of a goose. The goose was tightly swathed in a woman's large black shopping bag, which rested on the emergency fold-down seat at the end of the car. Then, looking down the packed corridor, he saw that it had taken on the character of a barnyard. Men and women sat on large wicker baskets, dozing or asleep, and nearly everyone had some animal beside him or on his lap. There were chickens packed against tureens of butter in the wicker baskets; the ducks and geese were wrapped in bags, with their feet folded under. Their heads and long necks stuck insolently out. From time to time, usually at a moment when least provoked, one of them would quack or cluck sharply. Fitted in with the passengers and the animals, nearly filling the space between the compartment doors and the side of the car, were large twenty-five-liter casks of wine.

The children looked up at him expectantly. He in turn looked at the conductor, and took Milou back in his arms. As for the barracks bag, which contained the children's things as well as his own — he would simply leave it where it was. The conductor seemed puzzled. "You are not with these children, lieutenant?"

"I am very much with them," he said grimly.

"And otherwise you are — alone?"

"Yes. Quite alone. And I'm afraid it's going to be something of a problem."

The conductor threw his arms up in a gesture of amused despair. "First a trainful of quacking animals. And now, as though that weren't enough to turn my hair gray, an American officer with four infants! It's not reasonable."

"It's not reasonable," Colvin said. "I'm completely in agreement. But have you any suggestion?"

The conductor frowned. "What can I suggest? We do not have trains like your American ones — with nurses and swimming pools and kindergartens. You are in France. There's even no place to sit down." He looked over his shoulder at the crowded corridor. "However, you obviously can't stand here all the way to Paris with this preposterous family on your hands. I'll have to make a place somewhere."

Colvin watched him balance and pick his way down the corridor. As he passed, the dozing passengers awoke sharply and stood up to let him by. He opened one compartment door after another, and Colvin heard him ask if they would make room for a desperate and overwhelmed American officer — a *très beau garçon* — who was escorting four orphans to Paris. Presently he saw people squeezing and spilling out of the fourth compartment; they were laughing good-naturedly. The conductor beckoned him to come over. As he worked his way down the corridor he realized that everyone in the car was talking about him; two women of forty, identically dressed in gray woolen sweaters, blue skirts, and heavy white woolen stockings, argued fiercely whether or not he was really an American. When he got to the compartment, followed by the children still miraculously hand in hand, he saw that only four persons remained: a very old lady in black, a smiling warmly wrapped couple of indeterminate age, and an athletic-looking country girl of twenty-two or -three with great muddy clodhoppers. The conductor explained that he had asked the girl to stay.

"You know children, mademoiselle?" Colvin asked hopefully. He helped the children off with their coats and folded them neatly in a corner of the baggage rack. The rack looked like the storage shelf of a grocery store.

"I ought to," she said. "I have nine brothers and sisters."

The three older children sat down side by side, not quite filling two places. Colvin sat opposite them, holding Milou tightly.

"You don't have to hold hands any longer," he said. The children disengaged themselves at once. Robert looked up at Denise earnestly. "Je m'appelle Robert," he said.

Colvin felt Milou squirming under his arm. He gave him a consoling squeeze. The child began to whimper. He looked up guiltily at the girl next to the window. She was laughing. "You'll excuse me, sir. But you can never hope to hold that child still all the way to Paris, four whole hours. He'll simply insist on a little climbing. Why don't you give him to me?"

Colvin handed him over with a sense of great relief. He was just sitting back for a much-needed rest when Robert leaned forward and tapped his knee urgently. "Je m'appelle Robert."

"Yes, I know," Colvin said. "And my name is Tommy."

The child continued to stare at him; his little blue eyes were worried. "Caca," he said.

Colvin raised his eyebrows. "Pardon?"

"Caca."

It was a very amusing little word. Colvin gathered that the child was imitating one of the ducks in the corridor. "Caca," he repeated after Robert. "Cacacaca."

Everyone in the compartment began to laugh.

"I'm afraid you don't understand," the girl said. "He means he wants to go to the W.C."

"Oh!" Colvin stood up, blushing. "I suppose he needs me to help him?"

She laughed again. "I'm sure it's not necessary. But I'll go along with him."

She got up and led Robert out into the corridor. Colvin sat down again, even more relieved than before. He remembered seeing the open door of the toilet when getting on the train. There had been three persons squeezed into the tiny compartment, such was the overflow of passengers at the end of the car. One man was sitting on the toilet seat and another on the wash basin; the third had perched himself precariously on the pronged receptacle for dirty paper towels. A goose squatted in a shopping bag on the floor. *Well,* he thought, *she asked for it.* And it was, after all, a woman's job.

The car jolted sharply. He looked out, astonished to see that they were still in the Auxerre station. But the train had begun to move.

He should have known that there would be people willing to help. In the end there were too many. For the first half hour they were content to crowd against the glass door to the corridor, smiling incredulously or pointing at him and at the children, who by now were more often sprawled on the floor than on the seats. But in the end curiosity and insatiable friendliness overcame their shyness. One by one they came into the compartment to ask why he was with four children, and stayed to discuss the von Rundstedt offensive or to ask how he happened to speak such good French. He could nearly always predict the course these conversations would take. Admiration of his perfectly tailored uniform would lead to the general remark that American soldiers were given everything they could possibly want, and this would inevitably bring up the outrageous pampering of German prisoners. Or, if the train slowed down while passing through a badly bombed railyard, the visitor would almost certainly cross-examine him on the inaccuracy of the Flying Fortresses. Many of them were seeing such wreckage for the first time; they stared unbelievingly at the charred locomotives shelved up on flat cars or on each other, the rails twisted into curlicue figurines as delicate as worked wire. Beyond the railyards were the rows of demolished houses, with now and then a single house or café miraculously untouched. If the town remained intact a quarter of a mile from the track, they agreed the work was well done.

The train sped through a frosted countryside. A red hazy sun hung over the trees and the flat fields; in the corridor it was very cold. But for the most part it was a good-natured as well as an exhausted crowd, and they were looking forward to seeing Paris for the first time in almost five years. At every station hundreds more got on, grotesquely laden with provisions for Christmas feasts: ducks, geese, and tubs of butter strapped to their backs, bombonnes of wine in their arms. They were dressed in whatever outlandish clothes they had left to keep them warm. Nearly everyone — former maquisards and stylish schoolgirls alike — wore solid hightop boots; many had heavy shawls wrapped around their waists under their coats. Middle-aged women with elaborate 1939 hats wore thick white cotton and woolen stockings that reached to their knees. It was the *exode* of 1940 in reverse, with the dive-bombers gone. Colvin was reminded of nothing so much as an expedition of skiers, adventuring into a frozen and unprovisioned land. He had enough friends in Paris himself; he felt almost guilty because he had not squeezed a goose or two into the barracks bag.

And yet, he had quite enough on his hands. The compartment was warm, and the children had drowsed off to sleep — except Denise, who stared at him with eyes that were beginning to close. Had he forgotten anything? He retraced quickly his steps from the moment when, happening on the name of the farm in his address book, he suddenly decided to take Jean's children to Sognac. He smiled, remembering the grandmother's bewilderment; and, after he had finally persuaded her, the frenzied hour of packing. He had assumed from the beginning that the rabbit-faced little maid would come along, but at the thought of spending a night away from the farm she had covered her ears and run from the room in terror. It was all he could do to persuade her to come as far as Auxerre — where, while waiting for the train, he had sent the telegram to Jantal, warning him to keep the secret. They had been outside the farm at five o'clock in the morning, waiting for the bus from Dijon. Behind them, in the lighted doorway, the grandmother waved good-by.

It was hard to picture Jean at that rambling lonely farm. Yet here, it seemed, he had met Anne-Marie. Was it a mistake, Colvin wondered, to have let Denise take the photograph along – that gentle face in which already a deep maturity brooded behind the almost girlish smile? He could not forget how, learning of his wife's death, Jean had torn up all his worn snapshots. Shortly before putting the children to bed the grandmother had taken Denise aside and had tried to explain. They were going to see her father, who had loved Mama just as much as she. And then, unasked, Denise had repeated the words over which she must have wondered often in those fifteen long months: "Tell Daddy I wasn't afraid. Tell him I did my part too." The four children had been taken to the prison, that last day. But it was only to Denise that the mother had spoken seriously, imploring her to remember those words.

He beckoned Denise to come over and sit beside him. He put his arm around her, and she looked up at him with her curiously patient little face.

"Are you glad you're going to see Daddy?"

"Oh, yes!"

"Do you remember him at all?"

She looked down at her feet. "I think I do. I try so hard. And of course I know what he looks like! We have a picture – each one of us." She hesitated. Then she looked up at him again. "It'll be like as if Mummy was here. Won't it?"

"Yes, Denise. It won't be like that at first. But after a while it will, when you get to know each other. When you're all living together again – "

"And you'll be there too?"

He looked out the window; and he wondered how he ought to answer that one. "No," he said. "Not all the time. Do you know what an uncle is?"

"Oh, yes! Like Uncle Charles. He brings us toys."

"Well, Denise, I'm a kind of uncle. So I won't be there all the time. But I'll come and see you now and then."

Her eyes had begun to droop again; her mouth fell open. He took her on his lap and, pressing her head against his shoulder, closed her eyes with his fingers very gently — as much as to tell her to sleep. And soon he too fell asleep: they had been up since three-thirty. When he awoke there was a great commotion in the corridor. The train was entering Paris.

It was just as well he had told them so often to hold hands. Four or five thousand persons, each carrying Christmas packages, must have poured out on to the single narrow platform at the Gare de Lyon. It would have been only too easy for one of the children to disappear among the suitcases, the geese, and the casks of wine. And the waiting-room itself was a madhouse: he would never have found them again. At the top of the stairway another four or five thousand persons were waiting, precariously held back to form a corridor by a detachment of policemen and soldiers. The chaos was increased by the fact that friends were meeting for the first time in two, three, or four years; the same gawky child of twelve would be recognized by a dozen persons. Or an aunt returning to Paris after four years would be astonished by the niece who came up to kiss her. The pimply little girl of fourteen was now eighteen and beautiful, very stylish in her remodeled hat and her high-heeled shoes. He saw at once that he would have to wait hours if he wanted to telephone. There were long lines before each of the booths.

In front of the station he stopped the first American soldier he saw—a reliable-looking T-5—and left the children in his charge. Then he went out on the street to flag a jeep or recon car that could take them to the office. There he would get a car for the day. He had to wait several minutes; even though it was almost noon and lunch time, there was surprisingly little American traffic. And there were of course no taxis at all. But at last an open jeep with only a driver stopped.

"Look," Colvin said. "I'm in a terrible jam. Could you drive me up near the Étoile? With a couple of passengers? I'm really stuck, or I wouldn't have stopped you."

The driver looked at his watch dubiously. "I'm late for chow already, sir. But I guess I can do it. If we don't get stopped too often by the M.P.'s."

Colvin slid into the seat by the driver and guided him back to the entrance where the children were standing. The soldier he had left in charge was giving them sticks of chewing-gum.

"Why should we get stopped by M.P.'s?"

"Oh, there's some kind of spy-hunt on. There's even an eight-o'clock curfew for soldiers."

Colvin got out and lifted Denise and Robert into the back seat. The driver turned around, open-mouthed with astonishment. "These the couple of passengers?"

Colvin grinned sheepishly. "There's four in all. But they really only add up to about two."

"But, sir, you know we're forbidden to ride civilians."

Colvin put Jean between the two front seats and held Milou on his lap. "They aren't civilians," he said. "They're children. I'll take the responsibility."

It was the first time the children had ever been in a car; they were breathless with delight. The driver lost no time: stores, cars, and all the noon traffic of downtown Paris streamed by as they twisted and turned. Once they were stopped, and the M.P., paying no attention to the children, examined their papers at length and then looked at their dog-tags. After that the driver twice turned sharply when he saw M.P.'s ahead; he didn't want to lose more time. Once on the Champs-Élysées, he took the jeep up to forty-five miles an hour, and this time Denise and Jean in the back seat hummed loudly, imitating the motor's sound. They were at the office by ten minutes after twelve.

Inside the elaborate building, with its marble lobby two stories high, he was struck once again by the incongruity: that an agency which had been parachuting men like himself into the darkness behind enemy lines, to kill or be killed, should now be housed in such ostentatious luxury. The guard with his white leggings, the elevator girls, and the polished information desk — what a long way they had come since the moment when he had closed his eyes and, counting *one two three four,* had jumped into the dark night! He had lain like dead, cursing the enormous parachute that bloomed behind him over two bushes, trying to gather it in, until out of the darkness a flashlight flared in his face and he saw, moments later, the terrifying unshaven faces of Morel and Jean Ruyader. He had been dropped at exactly the right moment; the French agent and his American sergeant, dropped so little farther on, had been killed. But he did not know this until later; fifteen minutes after his jump he had a glass of champagne in his hand.

He wanted to reach Johnston before he went out for lunch, to find out about his plane reservation home. But there was also the problem of lunch for the children. He couldn't take them to an officers' mess, after all. He left the children in the waiting-room and went down the hall to Johnston's office. There was only a W.A.A.C. in the room, typing at a small desk. She was a thin blonde girl of twenty-five, a corporal, and she had a pencil in her mouth as she typed.

"Major Johnston in?"

"No, he isn't, sir."

"I'm Tommy Colvin. I've got to see him. Do you know if he's in the building?"

The girl stood up, smiling. "So you're Lieutenant Colvin! I've heard so much about you. Major Johnston's out to lunch. As a matter of fact, nearly everyone is. They've put the lunch hour a half-hour ahead."

He thought quickly. A good responsible W.A.A.C. – if he could get her released – would take care of his problems for the afternoon – though what he really needed was a girl who could spend the night. He had a vague impression that there was a great deal to do about children at night.

"What part of the States are you from?"

"New York."

"Really? We're almost neighbors. I was at Princeton." He looked at his watch. "Look, what are you doing for lunch? Even W.A.A.C.'s have to eat once in a while."

"I was just going out."

"I know a nice little restaurant on the Rue des St. Pères – if we can get a car. Would you like to come?"

She smiled good-naturedly. "How many rules do you want me to break at one time? Eating in a civilian restaurant, going out with an officer, using a car instead of the Metro – "

"Oh, it's all right," he said. "Mme Morand's an old

friend. Besides, she'll put us in a room by ourselves. Not an M.P. in sight. And it's the best food you can get in Paris — "

"It sounds too good to be true."

He lit a cigarette, and offered her one. "Swell!" He helped her on with her coat. "And by the way, I'm afraid we won't be entirely alone."

He led her to the waiting-room. The four children were sitting quite still on the sofa. Then Robert got up. "Je m'appelle Robert," he said.

The girl smiled.

"Je m'appelle Mary."

Colvin looked over at her anxiously. Suppose she didn't like children? "You don't mind, do you?"

"Mind!" She bent over and picked up Milou. "Are you crazy? It's two years since I've had a meal with children. And as for lieutenants — they're a dime a dozen!"

It was a jolly luncheon. Once they had taken in their new surroundings, Mme Morand's own dining-room directly above the little café, the children began to babble incoherently of everything they had seen. Between long thoughtful spoonfuls, Robert presented himself again and again. It was Mary's first meal in a French restaurant, but she was so charmed by the children that she hardly noticed what she was eating, or that she had drunk three glasses of 1937 Chambertin. Colvin filled her glass as unobtrusively as possible. He was willing to use any means to seduce her — seduce her into taking the children off his hands for the afternoon.

As for the children, they were flattered by such attention and amused by Mary's queer broken French. He tried to see in their faces some mark of their ordeal, but they seemed no different from American children of their age—though Denise was perhaps older than her years. Without seeming to make a point of it, she was constantly alert, watching the other children. She would retrieve Jean's slipping napkin, or wake Milou from his day-dreaming at just the moment he was about to put the spoon in his eye. They were not small for their age, as most Paris children were, having spent the war years on a well-stocked farm. And there was a family likeness in those curiously patient yet contented faces. Jean was seven; though he seldom said a word, he seemed perfectly happy; he listened to everything that was said. Like Robert, he kept himself very neat. No doubt this was the work of Denise's training; she straightened her white stockings or collar every few minutes. Colvin thought of their father's unshaven face and dirty wrinkled uniform; and he hoped the combined efforts of them all would get him clean and sober for the children's coming.

As it turned out, getting Mary to take care of the children was no problem at all. He called Major Johnston after lunch; and once he had managed to convince him that he wasn't drunk, but really had four French children on his hands, he quickly got Mary permission to take the afternoon off. As for going home, he had a seat on Flight Seven for December 27: that was Wednesday, and it was now Saturday noon. He would get the children to Sognac Sunday night, or early Christmas Day if they missed the connecting train from Angoulême. It meant he ought to come right back himself, traveling on Christmas. He was supposed to confirm his reservation by telephone Sunday evening, and there was no telling how long it would take to call Paris from Angoulême.

It was Mary's idea that the children should rest at her hotel while he did the Christmas shopping and arranged for a room for himself. It would save a good deal of explaining at the billeting office if he didn't have four children with him. At the hotel he could slip them in easily enough. The Army was giving a Christmas party for French orphans at the Grand Hotel; Mary would take her charges there at four o'clock, and they would all meet in the lobby at half past five. He put off the problem of how to take care of the children through the night. Later, Mary could write out a list of things he would have to do. He seemed to remember that children had to be given daily baths.

Alone, an hour later, and with a billeting slip for the Crillon in his pocket, he could look around him for the first time. He went into the Café Wéber and ordered a glass of beer; except for tasteless "fruit juices" there was nothing else to drink. Then he walked to the Opéra, past Rainbow Corner, looking in the shop windows for presents for the children. There was almost nothing. A tastefully arranged window, gaily decorated with red, white, and blue drapes, offered little more than a few wooden soldiers. In the *confiseries* there were beautiful painted or enameled boxes for chocolates; but there was also a small sign saying that the next distribution of chocolate would be the 125 grammes for January. Four ounces of chocolate for a month! There were long lines at each tobacco store for the extra Christmas package of cigarettes, the government's gift of a third package for the month. The *pâtisseries* where before the war he had bought éclairs or fruit cake now offered a few small brown cookies topped by what looked like slivers from a pear. He walked over to the *Printemps;* there if anywhere he would find a good collection of toys. He bought four dolls with kinky paper hair, a small but accurately designed jeep (with wooden wheels that wouldn't turn), two bags of colored blocks, and a lumpy cloth ball; in a few minutes he had spent two thousand francs. He drifted aimlessly in the crowded store, and he began to listen to the people around him. They were talking of only two things: the Rundstedt offensive and the cold.

For after six days the offensive had not been stopped, and if the threat to Antwerp seemed less serious, one deep and widening arrow on the maps still reached for Sedan. The newspapers reiterated ominously that all communiqués were twenty-four hours behind the actual fighting — and how was one then to know if unchecked Tiger tanks had not already retaken Sedan? Once on French soil, and with the mass of the American First and Third Armies behind them, they might go on to Charleville and Reims; to Compiègne and Meaux and Paris. They would be thrown back in the end, of course; but they needed only a week to accomplish sufficient revenge. With a kind of helplessness Parisians spoke of the break-through in the Ardennes. They would have considered a collapse anywhere else less bleakly. But that the Germans should have pierced once again the same vulnerable little square on the map! It suggested that France would never be secure.

Colvin watched the discouraged faces of the crowd. For it was not the Christmas Paris had hoped for, in the first weeks, in the brilliant September days. He looked into the faces that hurried past; they were as grim as the faces of the soldiers squatting in the G.I. trucks that thundered by. In a few days Paris had emptied itself of the thousands of soldiers on leave. Watching them spew out on to the streets from the requisitioned hotels, staggering under their barracks bags and combat packs and rifles, it was easy to remember that sudden evacuation of another war: the army of jammed taxicabs rushed out to hold a crumbling line. They had come to think of the American army as an army perpetually on leave—holiday soldiers whose faces showed no mark of war. They had seen combat divisions only once, marching happily down the Champs-Elysées on the second day of liberation. They did not know that, except for that one occasion, these divisions had seen no cities at all, or had seen them only under fire. They had judged the entire army by a few hundred rear-echelon men. But now, watching the troops leave, they began to understand. The Americans might win the war with matériel, but it would not be with matériel alone.

As usual, large crowds of civilians had gathered outside the glass windows of Rainbow Corner at the Hôtel de Paris. A tall festooned Christmas tree stood just inside the door, and there was a dance orchestra on the bandstand, which had been redecorated for the Christmas parties. But there was no one dancing; there were only three or four soldiers in the coffee-and-doughnut line. The French hostesses were sitting in the large brown armchairs, talking or reading newspapers. Listening to scraps of talk, Colvin understood that the watching civilians would have liked to make some amends. They had thought, in their innocence, that the war was already over. And so for more than a month they had indulged in the kind of frank complaining that one uses with unquestioned friends. American soldiers were overfed, while the civilians starved. They had not suffered as French soldiers had suffered: look at their gay thoughtless faces, or only consider the way they treated Boche prisoners! They were money-grubbers: they sold chocolate, cigarettes, gasoline, even their clothes. They were an army on gay, disorderly leave. And they were cocky; they had never tasted defeat. There was scarcely a Parisian who had not said some of these things.

But now they had tasted defeat. There were still a few soldiers in Paris — the clerks and drivers and couriers attached to any rear echelon. In a few days they too, no doubt, would be gone. The civilians watched these soldiers hungrily, wanting to speak to them. As for the soldiers, Colvin thought he had never seen faces so forlorn. They wandered along the boulevards, singly or in two's and three's, looking for something to do. Depressed by the empty P.X.'s and Red Cross clubs, they queued up for the movies indifferently, or looked in vain for bars that still had some cognac and wine. Whatever celebrating they were going to do would have to be done before the new curfew hour of eight o'clock.

It was in a sense a colossal misunderstanding all around. The soldiers, self-conscious because they were so few, misinterpreted the glum faces of the civilians — a glumness compacted of anxiety and pity and, perhaps, a sense of having been unjust. Those anxious searching faces seemed to accuse the soldiers of having betrayed them by letting the Germans come back. As for the civilians, how could they mistake the sullen hostility of the soldiers, who for the first time in four months were making no effort to pick up girls? And the military situation must be really serious, if the soldiers looked so grim. They all knew the story of the German parachutists supposedly dropped near Vincennes, but it would surely take more than a few parachutists to bring about an eight-o'clock curfew. They would have liked to stop these forlorn little bands of Americans and invite them to have a drink. But instead they felt almost as far apart from them as from the strolling German soldiers of six months before.

So the two groups, the civilians and the soldiers, succeeded in lowering still further each other's spirits. And what a Christmas week-end it might have turned out to be if it hadn't been for the snowballing—for the plucky ingenuity of a few Paris girls!

No one knew just exactly how or where it started. Colvin, caught in the very beginning of it, could watch it grow. Perhaps a mischievous little girl in one of the dressmaking establishments, seeing a struggling and overloaded soldier, packed a snowball and hit him square in the face. Or two or three girls coming out of *Trois Quartiers* threw some snowballs at a lieutenant who was too well groomed. In any case, it started in that district, somewhere near the Madeleine. But within half an hour there was snowballing over half the right bank, as far up as the Étoile.

In the first minutes the girls, less timid, took all the initiative. Flopping in the high slushy banks of snow at the curbs of the Boulevard des Capucines and the Rue Royale, they scooped great wads of snow and packed them into hard round balls. It began with a few adventurous youngsters in bobby socks, but ten minutes later there were hundreds of girls whaling away: shopgirls and students and dignified married women. They would wait for an unwary soldier on the sidewalk, holding the balls innocently behind their backs. Or they would aim for a particular soldier glumly sitting on the strap at the back of a G.I. truck. The soldiers in the convoy, daydreaming of their lost Christmas, would be awakened by a splatter of snow; and a moment later everyone in the truck was howling with laughter. Little regiments of women stood outside Rainbow Corner, waiting for some hapless soldier to come out. They all found good targets in the white hats of the M.P.'s.

The snowballing spread unaccountably fast, like the sniping on the day of de Gaulle's first appearance. Caught off balance, the soldiers quickly organized in small bands. Presently snowballs were pelting down from the sixth stories of Army offices and requisitioned hotels. Individual soldiers hid in doorways, waited for girls to come out of the Métro stations. Then they would rush up and rub snow in their faces. And while the fighting went on, the older shoppers formed laughing circles to watch.

At five o'clock, when the long chow lines at the American messes began to form in the streets, bands of girls attacked in force. But many of the soldiers didn't bother to go back for dinner. The snowballing continued sporadically until dark, and for several days. But by dark on that first day there was scarcely an American soldier in Paris who did not once more have a girl on his arm.

When Colvin entered the Grand Hotel, at quarter to six, his overseas cap — which had been knocked off half-a-dozen times — was soaked through. He felt happier than at any time since the first days of liberation in Poitiers and Angoulême. Mary was standing by the door to the ballroom; she saw him first. Beyond her he could hear children laughing.

"I didn't have the heart to bring them out," she said. "Come on in and watch."

In the center of the ballroom floor, caught in a brilliant blue spotlight, a small and wizened fox-terrier was walking on his front paws, pushing an enormous rubber ball with his nose. In the half-darkness to the right an orchestra was playing "Sur le pont d'Avignon" in time with the dog's steps. And on the left, in a wide semicircle, were the children. They were sitting on little footstools, and each one had a large cellophane-covered basket of gifts. Behind the children the soldiers stood or sat cross-legged. Some of them were holding very small children on their laps.

Colvin tried to pick out the faces of his four charges.

But there was an expression of such rapt attention on every face that all the children looked alike.

Mary glanced up at him. "I don't know how to thank you for asking me," she said. "I wouldn't have missed it for anything."

He smiled. "You're not through yet," he said. "Do you have hot water in your hotel?"

"Let's see — this is Saturday. Yes, we always have hot water Saturdays. Why?"

He looked down at the floor, a little embarrassed. "Do you know, by any chance, how to give a child a bath?"

Chapter VI

At ten o'clock Jean awoke to the damp cold. He stretched out his right arm and felt the side of the bed. The edge of the sheet was stiff, moist, and almost frozen; he shivered. But almost at once he was conscious of unaccustomed warmth. Marthe was curled up to his back, her knees crooked into his; and he remembered how several times during the night, finding himself alone, he had pulled her to him. He relaxed against the warmth of her body: the solid warm curve of her stomach and the softer pressure of her breasts, the delicate warmth of her breath against the back of his neck. The warmth seemed a kind of protection against the soiled streaks on the ceiling, where water had seeped through during last week's rain; it protected him against the gray cold light at the window and the indefinable horror of the day.

He turned around slowly, so as not to wake her, and

looked down at her sleeping face. She was breathing very softly, her mouth slightly open. Her tangled brown hair was spread out on the pillow in a way to make it seem longer than it was. He leaned on his elbow, momentarily uncovering her left shoulder, and saw there a large and faintly purple bruise. Then he leaned over and kissed her firmly; her whole body moved. Her forehead knitted, and her face turned away with a tiny frown of disgust. But he understood that this was not for him. She was still asleep; and a kind of sickness crept over him at the thought of her going back to Henri. He closed his mind against the image of her nightly submission, the inert helpless abandonment to his hands. The little frown and the way she turned away from him when asleep told him all that he needed to know; told him far more than the single ugly bruise. She, who always looked so neat, must waken each morning to a feeling of being unclean. He kissed her again, gently, merely brushing his lips against her forehead. And then, when she made no protesting sign, he slipped his left arm under her head and cradled her in his arms. In a way he hated to wake her on this first morning together.

Sharply, he remembered the warmth of Anne-Marie: that somewhat slighter body in his arms. But this time, at the memory, he felt no recoil of anger; his whole body was relaxed in comfort and warmth. She was dead; but still he had no impulse to pull away from Marthe. And it was not merely comfort, for some of the tenderness which he had felt toward Marthe reached out and softened the memory of Anne-Marie. He closed his eyes; and these things drifted through his mind with the certainty of a dream. It was as though Anne-Marie were now reconciled to death; in the soft contentment of the sleeping girl's face, the dead face of his wife seemed submerged.

And he realized then what might happen with time. In her grave, submitted to the decomposing forces around, her body would lose form, until in some years perhaps it would be impossible to discern the bullet wounds. So in himself the sharp edges of memory might blur. The mind, having admitted comfort, can hardly turn back to its former way. And the time would as surely come when, persuading himself that Anne-Marie had achieved some kind of understanding in her last hours, he would feel no anger at all.

He now almost resented the peacefulness of Marthe's sleeping face. For have the dead then no claims at all? It was precisely in his own taut unrelaxing anger that his wife continued to live; tenderness would have been all right had she died a different way. Once he had tried to destroy that anger, the unreconciled fact of her death, by ferociously kicking the body of a German sentry he had killed. But he had felt nothing at all; only the strange heaviness of the body against his foot. There was no satisfaction – or there was satisfaction only in the sound of a sub-machine gun which, once he touched the trigger and for some exultant seconds, took on a quivering violent life of its own. He could lose himself in that sound. But minutes after, the twisting dissatisfaction would return – until one day he realized that it was good, a kind of loyalty, for the anger to stay alive.

For the final act was that her life had been cut off so sharply; or not sharply enough. She had not been given a thing necessary to dying: at least a moment's rest and understanding at the end. It was as though, in the act of letting her hand fall on a table, it had been arrested forever in mid-air; and in certain dark hours he could imagine her restless spirit hovering in the crowded air, eternally seeking a home. For what could she have known in those last hours but a desperate hoping for life, and then no hope, but only the unanswerable questions: What was to become of the children? What was to become of him? He had seen a man leave the maquis to go to absolutely certain death: his mission was to blow himself up together with a bridge so guarded that it could not be destroyed in any other way. He had not been flippantly heroic on leaving them, yet his face was deeply content. Of that consoling ideal, which he himself had felt only dimly and after many months in the maquis, she could have known nothing: the absolute certitude that in dying one was freeing many others to live.

She could not have known that ideal, simply because it could not be discovered alone. It had come to him in the long hours of talk in dark barns; in the sense of being surrounded by men who counted on you absolutely, on whom you could always count; in seeing the anonymous parachuted white figures descend out of the night — a comradeship that extended to the thin voices calling by radio from far-off lands. Perhaps the real explanation lay in this anonymity. In joining the maquis they had left their real names behind; and by that token had left behind their ordinary selves. In all those earlier years Jean had felt truly unselfish toward only one person: Anne-Marie. As for the others: he had watched their sufferings, he had commiserated with them — and it had meant nothing at all. It had taken this one kind of love to overcome self. Or it had taken an ideal born of suffering; something learned painfully, in separation from ordinary men.

He looked down again at Marthe; she was beginning to stir. If only Anne-Marie had died in any other way — Certainly it would be better for the children if he were to marry again. But as it was, it wouldn't be fair even to her. Poor Marthe! He had forgotten about Henri. She would have only two more days of freedom; and after that a kind of freedom only during the hours she worked in the café. And it was already ten-thirty, time for her to get dressed and go to work. After she left, perhaps he could go to sleep again. He put his hands behind her head and, kissing her firmly, woke her up.

Marthe walked happily along the unfamiliar street. A kind of inner music kept time with her steps. She was whistling while she walked; but not whistling aloud. From time to time the tune in her head changed its rhythm, and she wanted to skip to catch up. She had forgotten what fun it was to dance. But last night, when she closed her eyes and let Jean swing her around, it was as though her whole body had been caught up in the accordion's music. And she had only to open her eyes to see him there.

It was the first time she had been on that street in the daytime; the passers-by looked at her curiously, as though she were a stranger to the town. Lyon, Marseilles, Le Havre. She thought of herself walking down a street in one of those strange towns, Jean's wife, on her way to market for their lunch. There were hundreds of towns in France; hundreds of streets in each town. Lille, Nancy, Toulouse. In any of those places they would be strangers; it was only in Sognac that she wasn't free. They could run away to any of those places — or could they? Her whole life had been haunted by one daydream: a dream of running away. It had begun in school, when she was eleven years old, and the dream was so familiar (the little girl in black pinafore running, running), had buried itself so deep into so many years, that she couldn't make it take another form. Until she was sixteen she remained convinced that she would indeed some day run away. But in those early years there had been nothing to run away from; it was only as her life darkened and closed around that the dream came more and more to be nothing but a dream.

When she reached Marcel's, she was surprised to see Lieutenant Jantal and Yvette sitting at one of the tables drinking coffee. Beyond them Mme Marcel was at the kitchen table, peeling potatoes.

"Is that you, Marthe?" she called in from the kitchen. "These scalawags pounded on the door till I had to let them in. Eleven o'clock! It's no decent hour to be opening up a café."

Lieutenant Jantal was smiling broadly. He handed her a telegram to read:

ARRIVING SUNDAY NIGHT OR MONDAY MORNING WITH RUYADER CHILDREN HAVE ROOMS READY AND MEET ANGOULÊME TRAIN PLEASE DON'T TELL JEAN BUT KEEP HIM SOBER

TOMMY COLVIN

"How wonderful!" She read the telegram again. She could hardly believe her eyes.

"It was there when we got home from the dance," Lieutenant Jantal explained.

"But I thought he was going home – by the airplane?"

"He is. I suppose there's a waiting list, like for the Paris courier. He probably had to wait over a few days."

Marthe felt the tears come into her eyes. "It seemed such a shame Jean wouldn't get to see them."

"Well, there's no call to blubber now. He's going to see them. And you've got work to do, Marthe. You've got to keep him sober today. And keep him looking neat."

"Me?"

"Yes," Yvette said. "We've thought it all out. I'm going to take your place here, after lunch."

"Take my place? How can you do that?"

Yvette laughed. "All you do is look pretty and pour out glasses of cognac. At least I can try. After lunch he's in your hands till after the train comes in. We've got it all planned. You can go to the movie in the afternoon. The most he can pour down is two drinks during the entr'acte. After that, bring him back here to dinner. Mme Marcel's going to keep all her cognac for Christmas dinner tomorrow, so she won't have anything but wine here."

Marthe felt a little angry. They talked as though he were a common drunkard. "You don't need to worry so much. He only drinks because he's unhappy. He didn't drink much last night."

"'Love," Lieutenant Jantal said. "It's as good as cognac or religion to blind one's eyes. Or to cure you."

"No such luck," Marthe said. "But tell me, Yvette. How do you happen to be up and about so early? We came home awfully late."

Yvette lit another cigarette. Two of her fingers were dark brown from smoking. "I couldn't sleep. All night I woke up every few minutes. And I kept worrying. I don't want to spoil the fun, Marthe, but it was about you. I kept wondering where I'd seen your husband before."

"Oh."

"If you only knew the places he went, during the occupation! I was a courier for the maquis. I got all over France at one time or another."

"I don't know. You see, we weren't living together before '43. And even after that I never asked him. I was afraid to look into his life too closely. I was afraid of finding something I didn't want to know – something horrible."

"Yes?" Yvette looked very interested. "What sort of horrible thing?"

"Oh, I don't know. I really don't know! But when he

came home I could always tell when he'd arrested somebody. Or shot them, for all I knew. He'd have such a self-satisfied look."

"Limoges," Yvette said, half to herself. "Do you know if he went to Limoges?"

Marthe shook her head miserably. "I'm sure he must have gone to Bordeaux occasionally. He often came back with Bordeaux newspapers."

"That doesn't mean a thing," Lieutenant Jantal said. "You can buy all the Bordeaux papers here in Sognac. The *Petite Gironde* was sold all over the region."

"Why is it so important where he went?" Marthe asked.

Yvette hesitated. Then she looked up frankly. "I'm sure you won't be hurt if I say it, Marthe. If anyone ever looked like a *milicien* or worse, it's Henri. Now if I really did see him somewhere — It must have been something pretty bad, to remember his face so. If I could have him arrested, things would look a lot better, wouldn't they?"

"You're awfully kind, Yvette. But it's no use. He's not the sort to do anything in public — say arrest a man in the street. If he was that kind of collaborationist — and I don't *know* that he was — he would have been very careful about it. He'd never talk about the Germans with me."

Yvette shrugged her shoulders, dismissing the subject. "I suppose I'm just imagining things. I'm always getting hunches from people's faces. I guess they're usually wrong."

"Are you going to send Jean to the station by himself?"

"Oh no," Yvette said. "It would be much better if the children got washed up first. The train's due at eight-thirty. So around eight, Marthe, you get him out of here. Keep him away for about an hour. Then he can come back and find them all prettied up."

Marthe smiled. "I'm not sure I can move him around as easily as all that. But I'll try!"

After lunch Yvette washed the dishes while Mme Marcel plucked and cleaned the two enormous turkeys. From time to time Yvette looked over her shoulder at Mme Marcel, who had spread herself comfortably over a good part of the table; her fat fingers worked dexterously, and her massive sagging face had the expression of a pianist absently looking at the keys. They were alone in the kitchen, and there was only Mme Fougères with Mahmet in the front room. Thérèse had left with the Jantals; they were going to explore the near-by farms for butter and eggs and perhaps another *pâté de campagne*. As for M. Marcel, he had finally submitted to his wife's entreaties that he get his hair cut. After that he had other commissions; he had also promised to get two buckets of oysters. From the beginning they had planned a fine Christmas dinner. Now, since Colvin was coming back, they were going to have an apple pie too — if the Jantals found apples and sugar. Apple pie, M. Marcel insisted, was what Americans liked most of all.

When she had finished cleaning the turkeys Mme Marcel went upstairs for her daily nap. Yvette was glad to find herself alone. Or almost alone, for she could still hear Mme Fougères' nervous giggle from the front room. They would stare at each other, Mme Fougères and Mahmet, for perhaps half an hour without saying a word. He was a career sergeant, given to monosyllables; she was a university professor's daughter. They had nothing in common but the tiny room upstairs. At the end of the half hour Mahmet would decide to satisfy her and they would go up to the room; or he would walk away, almost without a word. The silence punctuated by giggles made Yvette nervous. She got up and closed the glass door that separated the kitchen from the bar.

So Jean was to see his children after all. She was glad; and at the same time almost afraid. For to see his children was almost like going home — the one thing they were all afraid to do. In the maquis they had talked so much of home in the first months, even in the whole first year she was there. But toward the end home had become something alien, like the tiny twinkling villages to which they had descended periodically on the food and tobacco raids. Gradually home receded into a beautiful and lost dream, the childhood fairyland to which there was no return. They still spoke of the same places with affection and pride: the rust slopes of Roussillon or the steep forested hills of the Corrèze; or the Étoile in a November dusk, as one walked up the Avenue de la Grande Armée. But how blurred those images finally became! All around them were the Poles and the Russians and Czechs who had not gone back from Spain, uprooted now for such a long time and so accustomed to maquis life that they had almost forgotten the desire to return.

She had always assumed that with the liberation they would go home at once. It was one of the things for which they had endured so much. But when at last they could walk the streets of Angoulême or Bordeaux without fear of being arrested, everything remained hostile and strange. For four years the towns had been in enemy hands; the towns had themselves been the enemy to distrust. Who now were the collaborators and who were not? Especially for those who, like Jean, had risked their lives every night, it was natural to think of nearly everyone as tainted. It was as though, walking those busy streets, they yet remained in their mountain maquis, aloof from ordinary humanity, contemptuously looking down. They had expected too much—and now they turned in disgust from a world where already the political squabbles had resumed, the compromises and rivalries, the good-natured appeasements. It was no wonder they didn't hesitate when asked to guard the Atlantic pockets, even though grossly underarmed. It meant they could hold for these few more weeks or months to their one certitude, the integrity of their own group. And now all these units were to be disbanded; scattered among the regular Army divisions, thrown in the teeth of the wind.

She heard a chair scrape in the front room and, looking up, saw Mahmet standing on the other side of the glass door. She started. For everything—the light and the size of the door and his position a few inches behind the glass—recalled the tiny observation room that overlooked the torture chamber of the Gestapo at Bordeaux. Stripped to the waist and sometimes naked, she had tried not to look at the faces that had stared down at her through the glass. In her humiliation she had tried to think of anything else, even of the methodical regular descent of the lash.

Mahmet opened the door and stepped down to the kitchen. "What's the matter? You look frightened."

"Just a nightmare," she said. "It's nothing."

"I want to pay for the two cognacs. It's twenty-four francs, isn't it?" He gave her three ten-franc bills. "Don't bother about the change."

She watched him turn and go out of the café, followed by Mme Fougères. Unreasonably, but still thinking of the torture chamber, she closed the glass door and locked it. She brushed her hand against her pocket to make sure her pistol was there; it was an old habit. Then she went back to the table and sat down. She put her hand on the plucked turkey; it was clammy and cold.

She couldn't get the torture chamber out of her mind. She shifted her chair so as not to face the glass door. Was it worth it, all they had gone through – and now that she could not forget? How many persons in all had been tortured, she wondered, during the four years – sustained by a mute heroism which they would simply have laughed at in '38 or '39? What had given them that courage, when now she was afraid even of being reminded, and foolishly locked the door? And Parisette, who every day had returned to the same room to be tortured on the hot stove, each time losing consciousness from the pain. But never giving away a single name. "Soyez une bonne française!" – the words, whispered in the darkness of the cell, had seemed to cancel out all Parisette's pain; even cancel out her own.

But was it worth while? For the terrible thing was that so many of those torturers were still walking about free; or had not yet been tried, after four months in prison. They would never know how many had themselves gone underground, or had crossed the Pyrenees into Spain. What if there really were a few white maquis in the south of France? And how many might not have infiltrated the police forces, or continued to get rich on the black market? Only an occasional sniper still reminded people of the *miliciens,* an isolated madman not to be taken seriously. These people, the ordinary timid souls who had never seen a torture chamber, had had enough of the *épuration.* It was something to read about in the newspapers, and now it was stale. They were ready to forget and forgive. Some day perhaps they would forget even Oradour-sur-Glâne. Yet all her life, thinking of Parisette or of those who had not come back to the maquis from reconnaissance missions, she would not forget. And she would not forget the sharp crack and tear of the lash: the sound a split second before the cut, and then the numbness spreading out into pain. More clearly than ever before, it was as though she were once again back in that almost bare room; the kitchen swam before her eyes until it had reshaped as the torture chamber. The walls had the peculiar sandy texture which they take on when one has a fever; the walls suck and close in.

She heard a sharp knocking on the glass. She looked up reluctantly, feeling the usual shame: the profound humiliation of her naked breasts. And she recognized at once the face of a man who had come twice before, almost certainly a *milicien,* though he was dressed in civilian clothes. He had been talking with a Gestapo officer behind the glass a moment before, but now he looked down at her with the faintest smile of amused contempt. It was almost a typical face, with its deep-set eyes, its perfect narrow mouth, its straight regular nose. And yet there was something about the face that set it apart from any she had ever seen.

The man knocked on the glass again. The illusion that she was back in the Bordeaux torture chamber lasted for perhaps five seconds, the time between the two rappings on the glass. Then her mind was perfectly alert, though she was fleetingly conscious that the palms of her hands were sweating hard. She was in Mme Marcel's kitchen. But the man was still there. And it was indeed the man who had watched her from the observation room in Bordeaux. It was also Henri.

So that was where she had seen him! The absolute nerveless cold of six months or a year before, when she had found herself in such situations, returned. She got up and walked straight to the door. Yet she had time to think – time to remember that she was alone in the café; that there was nothing to be done here, without witnesses. She touched briefly her pocket with the pistol; she would have to get him out of here, get him to the police station somehow. She unlocked the door, and Henri stepped down into the kitchen. He was smiling curiously.

"Excuse me," she said. "I was daydreaming."

"You certainly were! And why do you lock the door?"

She sat down on the kitchen table and lit a cigarette. If she were to offer herself to him bluntly? She could think of no other way. "I always lock doors. I don't know why."

He looked around the room, as though puzzled. "Where's Marthe?"

"Oh, she's gone to the cinema. There was a film she wanted to see. I took her place for the afternoon."

He looked at her, surprised. "That was nice of you!"

She would have to risk working so crudely that she might arouse his suspicion. She very deliberately put her feet on the chair; in doing this she slipped her skirt several inches above her knees.

"I can be very nice," she said evenly. "Especially when I'm lonely and have nothing to do."

He looked at her knees uneasily; and looked away.

"You're that Red Cross girl, aren't you? You know, I think I've seen you somewhere."

She was conscious of her heart beating very fast. But the coldness in her head remained. "Really? Maybe it was in Paris. I went to school in Paris during the war and the occupation."

He shook his head. "I didn't get up to Paris much."

She smiled brightly. "Well, it doesn't matter much, does it? Because we've met now."

She offered him a cigarette, and held up her own to

light it. He sat down beside her on the table. She was acutely conscious of her own absence of fear.

"I gather you're pretty bored in Sognac, if you spend an afternoon like this."

"I'm frightfully bored," she said. "You see, I came down to see a friend in the Air Force. He had set up a nice little apartment for us. But we had a quarrel. All I have left is his toothbrush and soap. Not that I cared much for him, but it's a shame for the room to go to waste. And when I have such a short time."

He looked sideways at her; and again she recognized the little smile of amused contempt. "You're a very pretty girl. You're also very innocent or very bold."

"Right now I'd say I'm being very bold." She looked him straight in the eyes. "Perhaps I'm hungry for a little pleasure. And then, too — I always make snap judgments!"

He stood up. "Look here, couldn't we meet some evening? If you're so bored — "

She shook her head. "I'm leaving tomorrow. And tonight I'm tied up. But if you'd like to come with me now — I'd only have to run up and tell Mme Marcel I'm going out."

"Excellent! This is certainly a stroke of luck for me — "

"Oh no," she said. "It's a stroke of luck for me."

She ran upstairs to Mme Marcel's room and told her that something so unexpected had come up that she would have to leave the café at once. She saw the irritated frown, but didn't wait to hear the protest. On the way downstairs she clicked off the safety catch on her little automatic.

He was waiting for her by the front door. "Where's your apartment?"

"It's on the Rue Provost de Sanzac. We go through the park."

He turned to her with another little smile; and she realized that his contempt was mingled with embarrassment. "I don't even know your name!"

"It doesn't matter. This is something that will begin and end this afternoon. We were both alone and bored. And we met. My name's Yvette."

"Mine's Henri."

"Yes, I know."

She led him around the Place François Ier. She walked quickly — and she thought of the number of persons they might run into who would spoil everything by their questions. They turned the corner, and she saw the flag above the police station, a hundred yards down the street toward the park. She calculated quickly. There was a Zouave standing in the sentry-box fifteen or twenty feet beyond the door to the police station. And there was a jeep parked across the street. A soldier was walking toward them from the headquarters building, seventy-five yards beyond; he was reading a newspaper as he walked. She slowed their pace a little, and she said nothing until they reached the door to the police station.

"Here we are," she said very loud. The Zouave turned around and looked at them curiously. Henri stared at her. "I thought you said Rue Provost de Sanzac. This is the police station."

"Yes," she said. She put her hands in her pockets; her right hand closed very slowly around the pistol as she talked. "We're going in here."

"But why?"

She looked at him steadily. "You know this building, don't you? But they don't know so much about you, even though I guess you worked here. The last time you saw me was in Bordeaux. In the Gestapo torture chamber." Her voice was very loud now. The soldier reading the newspaper hesitated and then stopped. "I was in the torture chamber. You were in the little glass observation room, looking in."

He stepped very close to her. The expression on his face hadn't changed. "Shut up, you little imbecile! You don't know what you're saying."

"Yes I do." She looked beyond him at the Zouave, who had started to approach them. "Are you coming in? Or do I have to call for help?"

She saw his right hand move leisurely toward his coat pocket; it was as though he were reaching for a cigarette. She regretted it in a curiously dispassionate way; she had hoped he had no pistol. *"Put your hands up!"* she said sharply. At the same moment he started to turn and took out of his pocket a small black automatic. Before he could turn back to fire, she pulled the trigger and fired three times. The automatic was still in her pocket; she thought absurdly of the holes she had made in her coat. Then she saw a kind of astonished expression spread slowly over his face; he turned away from her, and she heard his pistol clatter on the sidewalk. He doubled over himself as though he were going to vomit. She had shot him three times in the right arm.

When Jean and Marthe left the theater at five-fifteen, it was already getting dark. Their first impression was of coming out into a blustering storm. Vague black shapes streamed by them on the almost dark street, and there was a roaring sound like that of a train in a tunnel. Then they saw that these were more tanks, bearing down enormously as they swung around the sharp curve to the right and at once straightened out and accelerated for the open stretch ahead. Again Jean was conscious of anger tightening inside him. Were they bringing the whole French Army to finish a job they had begun with a few sub-machine guns and rifles, almost with their bare hands? What they couldn't have accomplished, with such matériel! It was one tank after another in a numberless procession, storming by at forty kilometers an hour and intervals of sixty meters. Then abruptly something struck him as very strange. The tanks were going the wrong way.

"I don't understand it," he said, looking at Marthe. "They're not on their way to the front. They're on the road to Angoulême."

"Maybe they're just practicing. Driving around the countryside."

Jean shook his head. They started walking back toward Marcel's. "Even they haven't got gasoline to burn. I can't figure it out. Unless — " He stopped dead. "Unless they're sending them back north to the Ardennes or Strasbourg."

"But they just got here. That would be stupid, to send them right back."

All cross traffic was stopped at the Place François Ier to let the convoy go by. A group of weapons-carriers and jeeps followed the first tanks. But they were driving at such speed that it was impossible even for pedestrians to cross the street. They went into the Café Glacier for an apéritif; and saw Bébé and half-a-dozen men from the Saujon group at a table in the back of the room. They went over and sat down with them. The men were looking very tired and dejected. Each one had three or four saucers under his glass.

"What's it all about?" Jean asked. "All that stuff going the wrong way?"

"What does it look like?" Bébé said. "They're going back where they came from. The Bretagne division's been recalled."

"They're going up to Belgium?"

Bébé frowned. "I don't know where they're going. The way the Boches have come back up there, they might be needed in several places. Perhaps in Alsace."

Sorel, who had been with the group since 1942, looked at his glass gloomily. "And that's the end of our vacation. We'll go back in the lines, of course."

Jean tried not to notice the look on Marthe's face. "Is it definite? You're guessing — or you know?"

"Know? I'm just a plain corporal, Jean. But I can use my eyes. If the division pulls out, we go back in. Somebody's got to be there."

"There are still the Spahis," Bébé said. "Nobody knows whether they're staying or not."

Jean ordered two Pinods. "So what? We're going back. I'm just as glad, myself. I didn't fancy ending the war driving a loud-speaker truck. What I want to know is, did they leave us any stuff? If they'd just leave us a couple of .155's — "

"They won't. An army doesn't work that way. They'll take the whole division, down to the last jeep."

"I'm fed up with it," Sorel said. "I don't want to go back."

"Nobody knows," Bébé said. "If the Spahis stay, they probably won't send us back. I don't think they could ever get the brigade really working again. If we hadn't had these days off, it would be different. But we've got used to sleeping between sheets again. We've let go. When you think you're through, you're really through. You're no good any more."

Jean shrugged his shoulders. "All we do is sit there. If we go back, we ought to attack. Even if we got half wiped out, it'd be better to attack than sit in holes all winter. And you can't tell. Just a little bombing might soften them up — "

"You're crazy. You've got to have something to attack with. Personally, I think the Bretagne division won't come back till spring or summer. And the whole war might end right here—in Lorient or Orillan or La Rochelle."

Jean got up and shook hands with them.

"It was nice while it lasted," Sorel said. "It was a nice thought. Christmas in Paris!"

They went out on to the street again. They waited about five minutes more, and then there was a break in the convoy and they crossed the street. They went directly to Marcel's.

When they reached the café it was to find the front room nearly full. Everyone in the room seemed curiously excited. Thérèse and Mme Marcel herself were serving drinks at the bar to several civilians who had never been there before. They wondered what had happened to Yvette—and a moment later saw her sitting at the table by the stove with Jantal and four other officers. They all looked a little drunk. Jantal got up when he saw them; his face was very flushed. "There you are at last! Have you heard the news?"

"About the Bretagne division?"

"Who cares about the division?" He turned to Yvette. "You tell them, Yvette. You did the work."

Yvette looked up at them. Her hair was tousled; her smile was very tired. But her voice was almost casual. "I had to shoot your husband, Marthe. Just a few nicks in the arm. Afterward I had him arrested."

Chapter VII

Colvin and the children didn't arrive until Christmas morning, by the eight-thirty train. The Paris-Libourne express, too late for the connecting train to Saujon and Sognac, had left them stranded in the Angoulême station at nine o'clock at night. There he was appalled to learn that the Bureau de la Place, which allotted all hotel rooms, was two miles away, and that in any case there were certainly no rooms left at that hour. They would have to stay in the station, but there were not even benches in the waiting-room. Some civilians wandered out into the darkness, hoping to find an all-night café; a group of sailors left in search of a brothel, where at least there were certain to be beds. But others simply sat down on their baggage, or even stretched out on the cold stone floor. Desperate, Colvin persuaded the sergeant of the station guard to accept them in the tiny guard-room. There was a small stove, and thin streams of smoke escaped past the lid. But at least they would be warm. There were six straw mattresses on the floor, with blankets and musette bags for pillows, but only four of the guards slept at any one time. Colvin spent the night dozing in a swivel chair or talking with the sergeant of the guard, but the children were tired from the long train ride, and they went to sleep at once. When they reached Sognac it was he rather than the children who looked more dead than alive.

Nevertheless they were rushed off to bed in the largest of the upstairs rooms. Mme Jantal had brought her electric heater to warm the room, and there had been stone hot-water bottles in the two double beds all night. Marthe had managed to slip away before Jean awoke; she fed the children hot milk as they sat propped up in bed. Then, while they watched her, not sleepy at all, she extricated their bundles of clothing from the bulky Christmas packages in the barracks bag, and laid them out. Denise watched intently for her mother's photograph to emerge, and as soon as she saw the leather frame asked Marthe to set it up on the table between the two beds. It was only then that she asked about their father, in a patient curiously firm little voice. Would they see him, perhaps, today? Marthe smiled, remembering how she had made Jean promise to shave.

Downstairs, Colvin warmed his hands over the stove while the Jantals told him about the arrest of Henri. Yvette had not got up to meet the train. But she would be there for dinner, and for the rest of the day. Colvin saw at once that he would never be able to get away before evening.

"It's too bad you're not staying for a few days," Jantal said. "I'm afraid this little Yvette is very fond of you. And she deserves some reward, doesn't she? It would be quite appropriate. Between the two of you, you've fixed things up for Jean and Marthe very well."

Colvin shook his head. "For one thing, she deserves something better than the few days it would last. You just have to look at her to know. She falls desperately in love, only to find three or four days later what a mistake she thinks she's made. She withdraws; it's always very humiliating for her. I'd not like to be a part of that."

"Then she's another war casualty? Like the rest of us?"

"Like the rest of us?" Colvin laughed. "The trouble with you, Roger, you've read too much depressing literature about the last war. You assume we're a lost generation, when we aren't even a 'generation'—yet! Take Yvette, for instance: her father was a director of the

Banque de France, wasn't he? Suppose she had remained a *jeune fille bien élevée*. Suppose she'd not gone into the maquis, but to a finishing school in St. Cloud. She would still have them — her hope chest of little taboos and inhibitions; and, having had no love affairs at all, she wouldn't have had any disastrous ones. Eventually she would have made a tawdry little marriage, very chic of course, with some other offshoot of the Banque de France. And she might have gone through life with no more serious mental disorders than ennui. Instead, what happened? For several years she lived among men — really accepted as a man herself. If it was at all like our maquis, she would never have had an affair, never have slept with anyone. No one would have thought of it. That was fine — but it was a kind of frustration, of course; an abnormal situation. And now, cast out into the world, and without her fashionable inhibitions, the years of frustration assert themselves. Sexually, she can't quite adjust herself."

"But on the other hand she's had the experience of the maquis?"

"Exactly. She has become somebody. She's had real friends; friends she would die for, if necessary. Do you realize how many attractive women have no true friendships at all? Her life, whatever happens to her from now on, will have had some meaning. The maquis may have disabled her for a quiet stupid conventional life, but also it gave her a character. It saved her from being nothing at all."

Jantal looked up at him curiously. "And you, Tommy, when you go back next week to your 'quiet stupid conventional life,' how are you going to find it?"

"I've always carried it with me," he said, smiling. "Didn't I give you a college professor's summary of Yvette? Any life is exciting, I suppose, if you have eyes to see. As for danger, I've had quite enough of it to last me the rest of my life; quite enough violence. When soldiers come home extremely restless, it's something beside a craving for danger they have to appease. The habit of danger, I ought to say. In a few cases it may be guilt – the Boches they killed. Killing a man is easy; one can be very impersonal about the body lying there. But afterward, looking through the man's wallet for papers isn't so simple. My God, what a lot of snapshots they carried on them!" He tried to turn the whole thing ironically. "Preposterously big families and whole litters of babies. It's so damned easy to reconstruct their squalid vulgar lives. Gefreiter Schultz posed proudly with his little blonde Elsa. And all oozing with *Gemütlichkeit!* Well, you can't help thinking of Elsa waiting for an answer to her letters."

"You're too soft," Jantal said. "You're like all Americans that way. You persist in thinking of them as human beings."

Colvin ignored him. "Or there's someone like Jean, with his helpless rage over his wife. The little girl insisted on bringing her mother's picture. I just hope it won't counteract the good it may do him, having the children here. You know, don't you, Jean threw all his snapshots away?"

Jantal nodded. "I remember. Jean found out about her death only a few days after I joined the Brigade. He tore the pictures to shreds. But he'll have to accept them sometime – things as they are."

"Now that Marthe's free – Henri may get fifteen or twenty years. Or he may be shot. We have enough from the same group to know about all there is to know on him. She's just what Jean needs, don't you think?"

"Maybe we'll know today," Jantal said. "But I don't

even know just what it is he feels about his wife. There isn't any way of telling, is there?"

Mme Marcel came into the kitchen from the hall leading to the backyard; she was carrying a basket of greens. She lifted the sheet that covered the small Christmas tree Jantal had bought the day before.

"What's the matter with you two good-for-nothings?" she said. "Do you expect those children to stay in bed all day? You haven't even laid out their gifts."

Jean leaned forward to look at himself in the mirror; he ran the tips of his fingers over his freshly-shaved face. And he wondered whether Marthe had the nagging habit. It had been only their second night together, yet she had begun to get on his nerves, reminding him so often to shave. And, pretending to look for missing or weak buttons, she had carefully folded his new uniform on the vanity table.

But after all, yesterday had not been any ordinary day; a good deal more than a little nagging might have been excused. In the first hours Marthe was dazed; she seemed unable to take in the fact of Henri's arrest, the fact that she was free. At dinner and afterward, at Marcel's, she acted queerly. Once, when the telephone rang, she ran to the receiver as though in a panic; she listened for several minutes, almost without saying a word. Then she put down the telephone and said to Mme Marcel, in a strangely disappointed voice: "He's not coming tonight!" Who was not coming? Mme Marcel had merely raised her eyebrows. Then, as the time neared when Henri normally came for her, she began to look nervously at the door to the bar, as though expecting him as usual. On the way with Jean to his room she had walked beside him in silence; and once, when he asked her how she felt, she said nothing at all. She clung to him with a kind of fierce silence, later, and all night she stirred in the bed. He awoke from time to time to her uneasy tossing. Something was wrong; or she dreamed perhaps that Henri would escape and find her. The last time he fell into a sound sleep; and he was surprised, when he woke up, to see that she had dressed and left the house.

There were still very few people on the streets: it was a cold bright Christmas day. He was uneasy, wondering why she had left without waking him, and he went directly to Marcel's. There was no one in the front room; he went back to the kitchen and saw Mme Marcel and Thérèse working at the large table, opening oysters. They looked up at him with a curious expression, and Thérèse began to giggle. Then he saw Jantal and, quite as though he had never left, Tommy Colvin! They were standing by a small green tree, and for some reason they looked very guilty.

"What are you doing here?" Jean said. "I thought you'd be back in America by now."

Colvin lit a cigarette nervously. "I had an extra day or two. So I thought I'd come back for a good Christmas dinner. And all kinds of friends in Paris who can't get away want me to buy them cognac. There's nothing to drink up there."

"Well, I'll be damned!" He noticed Colvin's two-day beard and tired eyes. "I see you had a time for yourself in Paris, anyway. You really look like a man who's been up all night."

"I have been up all night," Colvin said grimly. "That's not the half of it."

Jean noticed a dozen bulky packages, neatly wrapped, at the foot of the little tree. He touched one of them with his foot. "What the hell is all this?"

"It's a Christmas tree," Jantal said. "Some assorted Marcel nieces and nephews are coming in after dinner."

Jean looked at Mme Marcel; perhaps that was why she was grinning so. "I didn't know you had any nieces and nephews."

Mme Marcel jabbed a large oyster cheerfully and then worked it open. "There's a great deal you don't know, Jean."

For some reason they all began laughing. Then it abruptly struck him that Marthe must have said something. And where was she, anyway? "Where's Marthe?"

No one answered. Mme Marcel and Thérèse went on opening oysters. He looked at Jantal and Colvin; they were smiling again. Then that must certainly be it. But what could she have said? "Look," he said. "What's the big joke? Where did Marthe go?"

"I don't know whether you can see her just yet," Mme Marcel said. Then she did a very surprising thing. She got up from the table painfully, waddled over to him, and straightened his tie. She put her hands on her elbows, and he saw the same expression she had when M. Marcel teased her about leaving her to go to America — the tears behind her smile. "You're a good boy, Jean. You've really shaved and washed your face! You don't know how nice you look."

Jean felt very embarrassed. He wondered what Marthe had got into her head. *"Merde!* What kind of story has Marthe been telling you?"

Mme Marcel went out into the hall and shouted upstairs: "Marthe?"

"Yes?"

"Jean's here. Can he come up to see you?"

"Yes," he heard Marthe say after a few seconds. "I guess it's all right now."

"You can go up now," Mme Marcel said, turning to him. "She's in the big front room on the second floor."

He walked upstairs slowly. And he wondered what he could have said last night to Marthe. He had certainly not asked her to marry him. But had he said something to give her the idea — ? The door to the front room was open. He went in and saw Marthe standing by the window. She was wearing a dress he had never seen before: a black pleated skirt with a bright red jacket. It must have been an old dress she had outgrown, for the hem of the skirt came an inch above her knee. And he knew, seeing her there, that he loved her; that he wanted to hold her —

Then he was sharply aware of the four children watching him from the two double beds. They were sitting on the edge of the bed, with their feet dangling. *Four children* — He looked quickly at Marthe and then back at the oldest child. She sat primly with her small hands folded on her lap; and he recognized at once, despite her astonishing tallness, the high fine forehead and the blue lovely eyes. He suddenly felt very weak. He sat down on the straight-backed chair by the door.

"Denise?"

"Yes, papa!"

Then her eyes were dancing. She ran over to him and her thin body was against him, marvelously alive. Her tiny mouth was warm against his cheek and her hair brushed his forehead like soft threads of silk. He held her tight and was conscious, through the starched and yet soft dress, of the small perfect bones and the warmth of her body, the actual feeling of life. Then he saw, beyond her blond slight curls, one of the others jump off the bed and come toward him. "Je m'appelle Robert," this one said in an amusingly serious voice. Jean took him in his other arm — and again he was astonished by the sense of pulsing life, as though Denise had been a single miracle not to be repeated.

"But you've never seen Milou, papa!" Denise went over to the bed and took the smallest child's hand, as efficiently as though she were his mother, and brought him over to the chair. "He's so little he doesn't even know what 'Papa' means!"

He took Milou on his lap; he was surprised how heavy he was. And he was surprised too by the smallness and perfection of his hands – the tiny fingers, with the beautiful fingernails, curled over his own wrist. He knew at once, looking at that soft face staring wonderingly up at him, that Milou would be his particular favorite; he searched the face eagerly for what he could see there of his wife. Then a flicker of worry made him lift the child up level with his own head. He was certainly much too fat. His chubby legs seemed to burst out from beneath his tight-fitting suit, and his stomach was almost absurdly rounded, like that of an old man. He put his index finger on the child's wrist, so wonderfully soft, and after a few moments felt a tiny slow beating there. He looked up anxiously for Marthe and realized for the first time that she had left the room.

"What's the matter, papa?"

"But he's much too fat, Denise! He's as fat as a butterball. He's been getting too much to eat."

She laughed merrily, and patted his round soft knees and his wrinkles of fat. "That's the way he's supposed to be, papa! You've just forgotten. We were all fat like that, when we were little."

He looked down at Milou's bare feet, which stuck up so absurdly. He tickled the bottoms of the feet, and the fat toes wriggled. Because of this, somehow, Jean felt reassured.

"Are you sure, Denise?"

"But of course, papa! I know all about children."

Presently they were all sitting on one of the big double beds. He was not quite sure how they got there, but it seemed the only way to see all four at once. He kicked off his shoes and sat cross-legged at the head of the bed. Jean and Robert leaned on his knees; they stared at him as though their blue eyes would pop out. Denise sat beside him on one of the pillows, while Milou crawled excitedly at the bottom of the bed. And they all began to talk at once — telling him of the trip from Auxerre: the funny men on the top of the bus and the geese in the shopping-bags and the train and the ride through Paris. They went over in detail the Christmas party and the night in the station and the first night at the hotel. He listened to them in amazement; he certainly hadn't expected Jean and Robert to be able to talk so well. He turned to Denise, feeling proud of her because of the others — and noticed, on the bedside table, the portrait of Anne-Marie. He saw it obliquely; and looked away. It was a picture he had never seen.

"Was it a real surprise, papa?" Denise asked.

"It certainly was!" He kissed her high white forehead again. "My, you're so grown up now! I almost didn't know you — you're such a great big girl."

"I'm nine, papa."

"Yes, I know. And Milou's how much? He's nearly two, isn't he?"

"Yes."

At the sound of his name Milou looked up. Then he came over to Denise, and she ran her fingers through his tousled hair.

"It's almost like as if Mummy was here," Denise said happily. "Isn't it, papa?"

She reached over to the bedside table, picked up the portrait, and laid it on her lap. Jean watched her intently instead of looking at the portrait: Denise was looking at it with an affectionate amused smile, as though she were the mother and not the child. He knew that she must often talk to the portrait; he could tell by the way she held it.

"Isn't it, papa?" she said in a slightly worried tone.

Jean heard himself answer; it was like talking in his sleep: "Maybe she is here. Maybe she's watching us now, right here in this room."

Denise held the portrait almost to her face, and again she smiled as she might have smiled at a doll.

"Are you here, mummy? Are you watching us now?"

Then she laid down the portrait and crooked her arm in his. "I have a message for you from Mummy. She said it was very important and I was to remember it till I saw you. She told it to me that day we went into the city — the last time we ever did see her."

"Yes, Denise?"

"She said: 'Tell Daddy I wasn't afraid. Tell him I did my part too.' She said it to me over and over again. And she made me promise to say it every night, so I'd never forget."

He tried to fix his mind on something impersonal; on anything — the bedstead, the voices downstairs.

"And you didn't forget." He looked down at Denise's clear asking eyes. "Do you remember what Mummy looked like, that day?"

"Oh, yes! She was beautiful. And she seemed so proud when she said that: 'Tell him I did my part too.' But I've tried and tried to figure out. What did she mean by that?"

He got up and went over to the window. He looked out on to the bleak narrow street, and he waited desperately for someone to come out of one of the houses. He would watch him walk up the street, count the number of steps he took. But instead he went back to the bed and picked up the portrait.

"She meant lots of things," he said. "It's hard to say it all in just a few words."

But what did she mean? He had to ask himself this at last. Looking at the portrait he was struck by how different this was from the childish and terrified face he always saw in his dreams. He had forgotten; he was seeing again, yet almost for the first time, the deep calm of those level eyes. The portrait had certainly been made since his last visit home, in the summer of 1942; he had never imagined her since then except in tears. But she looked out at him from the portrait unafraid; there was almost a strength which he did not remember, from the Paris days. *"Tell Daddy I wasn't afraid. Tell him I did my part too"* — and for some reason he thought of the words of Yvette's seventeen-year-old friend in the Bordeaux Gestapo prison: "Soyez une bonne française." *Tell him I did my part too* — and sharply as a pain he understood how she had met her death. Almost at once he felt a kind of shame for the injustice he had done her — her and perhaps so many others too.

The realization crept in irresistibly. Supporting each other in the maquis, he and the rest, they had blown up the bridges and trains; they had been willing to lose their lives. And now they wore the uniforms and the brassards; they wore the right to judge and condemn. But how many others, outside the maquis, might not also have done their part? How many, tortured or threatened with death, had refused to speak — and had died proudly like Yvette's friend, though in a squalid dark cell? Anne-Marie had been a hostage, only one of many thousands outside the maquis to die by hanging or rifle-fire. The enormous fact crowded in on him. All these thousands too had refused to buy their lives. And so Anne-Marie. What had always obsessed him was the loneliness and bewilderment of her final hour, not understanding why this should happen to her, not aware that her death might have some meaning. But now he knew she had been completely aware; so aware that she had wanted him to know. Her final days, her final hour, lost in what she now understood, lost in the companionship of those who had already died, must have been the least lonely hour of her life. For it was this which had kept them going in the maquis, this unseen bond with all others who were fighting for the same thing; with all who were fighting alone and without uniform, in the dark. But now he understood how much wider that company had been, how in a sense it had included all those who had suffered and resisted as they could. In the suffering of all Frenchmen, though they may have remained in the towns and the unheroic valleys, they now could measure their strength.

He felt Denise's hand in his.

"What kind of things, papa? What did Mummy mean?" She looked up at him patiently. "Please try to say."

He sat down again on the side of the bed and put his arm around her. "She meant, Denise, that she knew why she had to leave us. Sometimes we do good and brave things, but we don't know why we do them. She was happy because she knew."

"And she's happy now?"

He looked down at those patient eyes, and felt, for a moment, almost the same faith. "Yes, Denise," he said quietly. "She's happy now."

Later, he took off his blouse and stretched out on the bed. The children were getting sleepy. Jean and Robert lay down on each side of him, while Denise busied herself tucking Milou into the other bed and whispering him off to sleep. He had closed the shutters, and the room was dark and warm — but not so dark that he couldn't see their faces. Across the room the red disk of the electric heater glowed softly. It made a pleasant hum. Listening to it and to the faint cheerful sound of the voices downstairs, he felt deeply at peace.

It had all gone so much more easily than he had expected, whenever he had thought of seeing the children again. Now, after less than an hour, Jean and Robert were completely at home: counting the buttons on his uniform, feeling in his pockets for his watch, or simply snuggling happily against his shoulders. He looked over at Denise, who was stroking Milou's forehead. Her curiously calm face stared down at the baby gravely — he could think of Milou only as "the baby." But had it not been for Denise's thin legs dangling over the side of the bed, and her black buckle shoes, she would hardly have seemed a child. He knew it was because of her that things had gone so smoothly; somehow, she had prepared the others for him. And it was because she was so strangely mature that he could believe the message from Anne-Marie. For she had remembered not only the words; she had remembered also how proudly her mother had said them. She seemed almost to relive, in her child's face, that pride; that quiet courage and calm.

There were problems, of course; some day he would have to worry about these things. But how much better it was to have such problems than to live over and over again the same indefinable torments, the useless self-questionings. Even to run the problems over in his mind couldn't trouble this deep sense of peace, this feeling that he had almost forgotten of the body and mind at rest.

How were they going to live? And where? He rebelled at the thought of sending them back to the farm: yet in two or three days the Brigade might go back into the lines. Suppose his mother-in-law died — what would happen to the children then? If the Spahis stayed at Rujon, he would probably be stationed at Sognac with Jantal; it would be much simpler that way. But Rujon or Sognac, and even if Marthe or Mme Jantal were willing to take care of the children, how could he support them on four thousand five hundred francs a month? For the first time in four years he felt himself again; but it might be years more before he would be out of uniform and making a decent living. He might even be sent to the Pacific. He felt the weight of these things; they crowded in on his mind. Yet deeply beneath them the sense of peace remained.

He no longer doubted: some day he would marry again. For Denise, competent as she was, was still a nine-year-old child. Robert and Jean had fallen asleep; Denise had crawled under the covers with Milou. He picked up once again the portrait of Anne-Marie; and, looking at it, he knew that there was no longer any reason why he shouldn't marry again, unless it lay in some obscure kink of the children's minds. He loved Anne-Marie as much as ever, and in a way that would deeply affect any other love. But now for the first time, because her life had achieved a kind of completeness, she seemed to him truly dead. The part of her that lived on was at peace.

He knew without looking that Denise was still awake; even that she was waiting for him to speak.

"Denise?"

"Yes, papa."

"Come over and sit by me."

She slipped out of the bed and curled up at his feet, leaning on his crooked-up knees. He picked up Robert gently and lifted him over by Jean, so as to make room for her beside him.

"That's nice," she said. "Nice and snug and warm."

"You're quite a little mother for the others. Aren't you, Denise?"

She smiled brightly. "Oh, they're very good. They do everything I say — most of the time."

"And you know just what to say!" He kissed the tip of her nose. "But did you ever think about having somebody else, a little like Mummy, when we all got together?"

"Oh, yes! That was another thing Mummy said when we saw her. She said when we found you we'd have another mother — a kind of mother — to look after us." She laughed gently. "She said you were very hard to take care of, papa. She said I couldn't do it all by myself."

"Mummy liked to tease," he said. "I'm very easy to take care of. But if you had another mother, Denise — you'd have two, wouldn't you? Not just one."

"Yes. But Mummy said after a long while we'd all be together again. Everybody."

"That's true. That's the way it'll be."

He looked again at the photograph of Anne-Marie. How much she had thought of, that last day!

"Is she here, papa?"

"Who?"

"Our new Mummy? Will we see her today?"

He reached into his pocket for a cigarette. He lit the cigarette and showed her how the lighter worked. But he knew she was waiting for an answer.

"Maybe," he said. "But there are all sorts of nice things happening today. And a great big Christmas dinner! You don't want everything at once, do you?"

He got up from the bed and slipped on his shoes.

"Shall we get dressed too?"

He bent over and kissed her again. "You better sleep a little more, pet. You've got a long day ahead."

He closed the door softly behind him and went downstairs to the kitchen. Colvin and Jantal had left, but Marthe was there, hanging ribbons on the little tree. She bent over to move one of the packages, and he saw a card: "To Denise from Papa." She looked up at him, and brushed away a long falling lock of hair. His voice was almost harsh: "Come out in the hall a minute, Marthe."

She followed him out into the narrow hallway.

"How do you like them?" she asked.

"They're wonderful, of course. But how do *you* like them?"

"Oh," she said. "I think they're the nicest children in the world."

He looked at the wall behind her. "I'm glad you think so. They're much too much for me to take care of. I can't have all those children on my hands."

She smiled. "What do you want me to do? Adopt a couple?"

"No," he said. "I want you to marry me."

Somehow Mme Marcel had miscounted: they were fourteen at table in the end. However, the children more than absorbed the extra place, since they wanted to take their new dolls to table with them. Milou held his cloth ball on his lap. The long wide table seemed to slope dangerously down from the end near the stove, for at that end were not only the great brown turkey and the platters of vegetables and potatoes, but also the enormous Marcels. The Marcels, the Jantals, and Colvin thus took up half the table; the other half was given over to the children and the dolls. On one side little Jean and Robert sat between Mme Jantal and Yvette; on the other side Denise and Milou were between Marthe and Jean. Thérèse ate at the foot of the table and also did the serving.

They were at table almost four hours. Watching the first darkening outside, Colvin tried not to remember that it was his last real dinner in France, his last meal *en famille*. Tomorrow he would have a few sandwiches on the train, and after that it would be the gloomy officers' mess in Paris. He thought of his first dinner in the maquis: the farmhouse attic decorated with French and American flags, and the twenty-five or thirty bottles on the table. Then, too, they had been at table four hours; every half-hour someone would come in to report that the two men who were dropped from the same plane had not yet been found. He looked around him at the bright kitchen. It could not have had a better end, the two years which had begun with that terrified jump into the dark night. He loosened his belt again and let his mind run pleasurably over the grotesque amounts they had eaten: the oysters and the steamed clams; the soup and the *pâté de foie gras;* the *pâtés de campagne.* Then the turkey with its chestnut dressing, the superb *purées,* and the salad—and even the special present for him, a deep-dish apple pie.

Naturally after such a dinner they began to sing. At first Jean or Yvette merely started the tunes, and the others would take them up—wistful yet happy songs of Paris or the maquis. But later Jean sang long humorous narratives alone, and as he sang he circled the table, returning with each chorus to stand behind one of the children's chairs. They were delighted: it was no small discovery to learn that one's father could do such things! They in turn had their own surprise, when Denise stood up and sang "En passant par la Lorraine" in a bright treble; with every chorus Jean and Robert and even Milou joined in, tapping their shoes on the floor:

. . . oh oh OH, avec mes sabots!

Colvin himself had a very bad five minutes when they insisted on "The Star-Spangled Banner," and he couldn't remember all the words.

He watched Jean and Marthe closely. And he knew that they had come to some kind of understanding, though they said nothing. Perhaps she was on trial before the children; if so, it was clear enough how the judgment would stand. They loved her already. As for Jean, it was astonishing how much in these few hours he had changed. He lolled back in his chair easily; his sudden flaring anger, his unaccountable changes in mood were gone. And even the Jantals had not quarreled once.

He looked at his watch; Réné would come by any minute now with the car. And it was perhaps better so. He knew that this last impression would in a way be false; life rarely offered one such an opportunity to bow out of it at the height of a Christmas mood. He would go back home to his old life; when he got up from the table it would be to draw a curtain over these two years of his life. But behind him, behind the curtain, the dark insoluble problems would remain. He would carry with him the knowledge that most of France was starving, but he could also remember, symbolically, this one afternoon. And so too, after he had left, the Jantals would go back to their room – to resume their bickering, helplessly trying to bridge the gulf that fifty months' separation and prison had cut. He shook his head, as though to drive out the thought of their failure. He would leave; he could remember them as they were today.

Then he heard the front door slam and Réné had

come for him, to drive him to Angoulême. They followed him out to the car, but he wouldn't let them get in to come along. He wanted to think of them in the café together, after he had left. He said good-by almost casually; it was a kind of pretending that he would see them all again.

On the way to Angoulême they hardly talked at all. And through the long day no one had said anything about the news that had become definite at last: the Brigade was going back into the lines. He knew nothing about it at all until late the following day, in Paris, when he paid a routine call at French Army headquarters to check out.

Chapter VIII

From his desk near the window Colonel Ruc watched the men come back. He could see them through his half-open office door, staggering into the dark hall under the weight of their rifles and improvised barracks bags. Someone was trying to start a fire at the other end of the room, which they used for their mess. Or, leaning far back in his chair, he could look out the window and see them arrive outside: seven or eight to each civilian sedan, twenty-five or thirty to each gazogène truck. The men let themselves down wearily from the trucks on to which they had climbed so eagerly only a few days before. All night, men would be coming back; he could count on at least four or five truck breakdowns between Sognac and Rujon. And once again they would have to use their ingenuity where they needed tools and spare parts. To the last jeep and weapons carrier, the two motorized divisions were gone. They had left no trace but the high mound of empty K ration boxes in the headquarters backyard.

In the hall the men were lined up to give their names to Captain Morel; some of them had checked out with him only twenty-four hours before. For so it had been: the last outposts had just been relieved when the final orders came, taking away the Spahis and sending the Brigade back into the lines. On the entire front and as far as Sognac the two convoys must have crossed incessantly on the road: the sleek uniform tanks and armored cars of the Spahis; the returning civilian sedans and limping gazogènes of his own Brigade. He had seen them leave, the two crack divisions — the men disappointed to be going back before they had liquidated Orillan; yet a little proud to be snatched from the task, caught up in the urgency of their rescuing flight across France. But his own men, who had got no farther than Sognac or Saujon, were returning merely to stand guard. They had waited for months for arms, but now they knew exactly where they stood. In due time, when they could be spared, full motorized divisions would again be sent down to finish off the German coastal pockets. It was not to be their own job, the actual taking of Orillan.

He watched the men sitting on their barracks bags, or getting down from the trucks into the dusky street. They had done nothing in their two or three days at Saujon. The bars closed early; there was simply nothing to do. Yet they seemed much more tired. The relaxation had sapped their strength. Under the belief that the job was done, their long-held last reserve had collapsed. He wondered whether he would ever be able to work them into a fighting unit again. So long as the Brigade remained a brigade, some intangible of morale had overlaid their individual weaknesses: the years of fatigue, the men who had been wounded too often, the men who were simply too old. But the very act of their disbanding had destroyed that force. The burden itself had carried them for months; but they had let it down as a weight never to be taken up again.

And yet he would have to do something. It was small comfort to know that the morale of the pocketed Germans, five and ten miles beyond those frozen marshes, was also low; some other intangible still made them resist. Was it the dramatic consciousness that they were five hundred miles behind the Allied front lines? Or was it the consoling sound of the courier plane from Berlin, a nightly witness that the Fatherland had not forgotten them, knew of their heroism? Reasonably, they should have surrendered months ago. In September and October they had waited for an American army to appear; they would not surrender to the F.F.I. But this was the twenty-seventh of December; they knew well enough now that not a single prisoner had been killed. And in those months, in spite of the raids and the boats from Spain, their food-stocks had begun to run low. Their commanding general had left for Berlin a month before, disappearing one night by the courier plane. They had every reason to surrender. But it looked now as though they were determined to stay there till the end of the war.

He got up from his desk and went over to the door. Some of the soldiers at the end of the line, seeing him there, saluted; others, who had taken off their caps, grinned ruefully or shrugged their shoulders, as much as to say "C'est la guerre!" But they remained flabby and spiritless behind these courageous sallies. He was the more startled to see Jean Ruyader at the very end of the line, obviously in high spirits. Seeing him, Jean came over and saluted. He was well-shaved; even his uniform was clean.

"Well, Jean," he said. "You don't seem sorry to be back."

"I'm not. I didn't like the idea of being just a driver. And I guess I didn't look forward to all the regular army *chi-chi.*"

Colonel Ruc looked at him squarely. "You take it very well. I know you had your heart set on seeing your children."

"Oh, but I saw them! Tommy Colvin brought them down. They're in Sognac now."

"Splendid!"

"Yes. Mme Jantal and a little friend of mine are looking after them. They're quite something."

"Lieutenant Colvin's been a pretty good friend," Colonel Ruc said quietly. "From the beginning to the end. He stayed with us till he thought it was all over. It's not going to be the same without him."

"Yes," Jean said. "We decided not to tell him—even when we knew we were coming back. He'd worry about it."

Jean went back and took his place in the line. Colonel Ruc walked slowly toward the table where Captain Morel was taking the names. Because the men looked so tired he thought it better not to stop and shake hands with any of them. He leaned over Captain Morel's shoulder and looked at the list. "How many of the men are back?" he asked. "There's forty or fifty in line."

"I don't think there'll be many more tonight. The rest probably couldn't get transportation. Or the cars broke down on the way."

"All right. Stop taking names for a few minutes." He smiled a little grimly. "For what it's worth, I'm going to make another speech."

The men who had already been through the line were lounging at the dinner-tables or sitting cross-legged on the floor; they were waiting to form for the return to their posts. He worked his way through them until he had reached the fireplace. Then he turned and faced them. They looked up at him patiently; and he was conscious more than ever of their fatigue. They even had no longer the strength to be angry because no heavy guns had been left them. They simply didn't care any more.

But he began quietly. Whatever they might need, he wasn't going to make a fiery speech. They had been together too long for that.

"Gentlemen. When I last talked to you, I thought I was talking to you also for the last time. Two nice bright shiny armored divisions had come down to relieve us; and we were to go for a rest. We were, if you like, thrown out. We were going to regular army schools: to become cooks, or clerks. Or even 'soldiers.' We were going to learn to salute and march and make beds the army way. Perhaps this hurt our pride a little. But we were glad all the same. We were going to sleep in warm barracks and get passes to Paris. We were going to get a rest. And God knows we needed, after four years, a little rest. So far as we were concerned, Orillan was over, the Atlantic front was finished. We were going to be part of something else. It had become somebody else's war.

"That's the way it was about a week ago, when we had our last dinner together. We drank up the champagne — because our part of the fight was finished. But here we are back. We were wrong. The fight was not over for us. And tomorrow night we'll be back in the snug foxholes and the nice warm patrols. A good many men are already there. And there's no more champagne to drink.

"In a way, this was my fault. It was my job to know it wasn't over. Because it was a very big mistake that a lot of us make. We work hard and go on our patrols and perhaps get wounded; and then, because we're relieved or the enemy surrenders, we think we're finished, we think the war is over. But I want you to realize, gentlemen, that our particular fight is never over. The things that this maquis – this Brigade – was formed to fight are going to continue to exist, long after Orillan surrenders; long after Germany surrenders. A good many of you have been fighting these same things for around ten years. You began in a civil war in Spain, and now you're in one small part of what's called a world war. But I don't need to tell you that it's the same war. I only need to remind you that there is always, somewhere, a civil war. And that war is always going to be the way it was in Spain. You're going to have Spaniards on both sides. You're going to have Yugoslavs and Americans on both sides. You're going to have Frenchmen on both sides.

"Now, this is what I mean about a civil war. You're tired tonight. You've come back to hold in a German garrison that has more arms than you have. More, because you've almost none at all. You may have the feeling that you've been deserted, forgotten on your small front, left alone. It's easy – here in Rujon – when you read about Strasbourg and the Ardennes, to feel very much alone.

"What I am trying to say is that we're not alone. We're no more alone than the unarmed Chinese partisans or the unarmed resistance in Warsaw were alone. We're no more alone than the *guerrilleros* in Spain today are alone – for all over the world there are tired and unarmed soldiers, there are civilians even, who think the things we think; who know they're fighting in a civil war. It's this thinking the same things that keeps us from being alone. And this civil war will be won not by .155's and planes only. It will be won by thoughts like ours; by men like ourselves. And then, when we have the illusion that the civil war has been won — then is the time to watch out. For it will already have begun again."

The words had come easily; but now, abruptly, he didn't know how to go on. The faces of the men stared back at him: some of them expectant, some merely tired. It had been, perhaps, too general a line to take. He had tried to give them a consciousness of men all over the world fighting for the same things, the bond between them, when what he needed to restore was that smaller bond that for four years had held them together.

"You're very tired tonight. You may feel that you have never been so tired. But I want to remind you of one or two other occasions when we were also very tired; when we thought we had nothing left."

But even this seemed a bad line to take; it would merely depress them to remember those nights and days. He looked again over all those faces, almost stubborn in their fatigue. And then he saw, standing in the doorway to his own office, a man in an American uniform. He looked again. It was Tommy Colvin.

What was he doing there? He should have left for America by now. Colonel Ruc kept staring at Colvin. He could not look away, and he realized sharply that he had forgotten what he was saying. He didn't know how to go on.

Then he was aware that the men facing him, seeing his own stare, had begun to look around. Some of them were standing up.

"Go on, colonel," Colvin said. "Excuse me for coming in late."

"What are you doing here?" Colonel Ruc asked. "I thought you'd gone." His voice was sharp, as though he were delivering an official reproof.

Colvin smiled. "I did go. But I checked out at G.H.Q. in Paris, of course. And there I heard that everyone in the Brigade was ordered back to Rujon."

There was a long silence. It was Colvin who finally broke it once more. His voice was almost angry:

"Well, what the hell, colonel? Do I belong to this Brigade or not?"

Cognac-Verdun
December, 1944–February, 1945

Afterword

Maquisard: A Christmas Tale, more than any of my other novels, was closely based on personal experience and a real historical situation. At the time of my stay with the French, in the icy December of 1944, the Royan front was at a stalemate, while the French waited for the weapons needed to liquidate the German garrison. There were skirmishes, with minor raids from both sides, but no definitive action.

In my short stay in Cognac (the "Sognac" of the novel) I formed several warm friendships, one of these with the original of Jean Ruyader, the maquisard of the title.

I was in Cognac on the quixotic mission of instructing the French in American psychological warfare methods, specifically in the use of a "398" loudspeaker truck that would broadcast surrender appeals to the beleaguered Germans. The truck's loudspeaker had been used with remarkable success at the port of Brest, inducing a peaceful mass surrender. My mission was quixotic because I had no experience with loudspeaker appeals and had never even ridden in a 398. My work, prior to the liberation of Paris, had been in political intelligence, trying to determine who was and who was not reliable in newly liberated towns. Later there were special missions: one to track down 26,000 Spanish anarchists who, as it turned out, did not exist; another, for the OSS, to investigate conditions in southern France.

The 398 loudspeaker never arrived, and in late December I was, like other detached personnel at the time of the German counteroffensive in the Ardennes (the "Battle of the Bulge"), recalled to my company and stationed in Verdun for possible transfer to the infantry. This transfer never occurred, and during the ensuing weeks without an assignment I wrote *Maquisard,* moving from typewriter to typewriter whenever one was free. I finished it in less than a month. With the end of the war in France I was again detached from my company, this time to work in the cultural relations section of the United States Information Service in Paris.

There was organized resistance in France from the first hours of the debacle of June 1940, but the first substantial maquis developed in 1942, with many of its recruits escaped prisoners of war or fugitives from the German forced labor battalions. There were also a good number of foreigners in the maquis, including veterans from the loyalist forces of the Spanish Civil War. It was to the maquis that the British Special Operations Executive and the American OSS parachuted arms and special agents, often accompanied by a French native. British-American-French parachute teams known as "Jedburghs" were active in 1944; each team had a radio operator who could communicate intelligence to headquarters in England.

In Lieutenant Colvin I had in mind a particular officer much admired by the French soldiers I knew in December 1944, the journalist Stewart Alsop. I never met him, as he was not in Cognac, and only this year read his 1946 book *Sub Rosa,* now out of print. It describes a "Lieutenant Wheeler" parachuting to a maquis, where he was warmly received. Alsop's account evokes the tight bond of courage and loyalty among men risking their lives in guerrilla action, usually with meager and antiquated weapons. Some of these were relics of the Spanish Civil War—in one instance a rifle dating from the war of 1870.

The inevitable revisionism has cast doubt on the efficacy and heroism of the French Resistance. I believe *Maquisard* is historically accurate in its picture of the military situation, of the courage and patriotism of the resistance fighters, and of the way men and women felt in the discouraging hours of December 1944.

The novel has two themes. One—the difficulty of readjustment to civilian life—is only too familiar to Americans still traumatized by the Vietnam war. The men who had risked their lives in the maquis, and who now had little to look forward to, felt alienated from the civilians who were resuming their normal lives as though nothing had happened. How could one tell which were the patriots and which were the collaborators? Naturally, there was widespread resentment and distrust.

The second—the aversion of the resistance soldiers to being absorbed by the regular French army—may require some explanation. By the end of 1942 there were a number of secret resistance groups operating independently of each other, some in Paris and other cities, some in the country. All were engaged in harassing the occupier. One of the most active was the FTP or *Francs Tireurs et Partisans Français*. Communist dominated at the top, it included veterans of the Spanish war and other foreign soldiers. The men I knew in Cognac, a number of them from the FTP, were fairly apolitical, although vaguely leftist and still imbued with the socialist, egalitarian ideals of the Popular Front. They were also intensely patriotic, ready on the slightest pretext to break into the *Marseillaise*.

Some maquis brigades belonged to the national FTP organization; others were Gaullist, guided more than the rest by instructions from De Gaulle headquarters in London. By 1943 (and even more by early 1944) it seemed important to absorb the various resistance military groups into a national underground army, the FFI (*Forces Françaises de l'Interieur*). General de Gaulle, and with him the American and British high command, recognized the invaluable help of resistance forces on the eve of the invasion. But they were uneasy at the thought of small armies still operating independently. They were particularly reluctant to see the FTP heavily armed. Wild rumors abounded, even one of a "Socialist Republic" in the department of the Haute-Vienne, rumors as unfounded as the one of my 26,000 Spanish anarchists. But De Gaulle and the allied leaders were right to want coordinated action and a single high command on the eve of the allied invasion.

There was some sense of loss but no prolonged resistance when the proud individual brigades and maquis were absorbed by the FFI. For at least they could now hope for decent uniforms, more modern equipment, and hope too that the American army would supply artillery and tanks. The next step, however, was for the FFI to be absorbed by the regular French army, some of whose officers belonged to units that had fought recently in North Africa. But other officers were *napthalines,* i.e. men who had not participated in the resistance and whose uniforms had been in mothballs since the debacle of 1940. These veteran officers now insisted on all the military formalities from constant salutes to close order drill. The old comradeship of the maquis, with officers and men on an equal social footing and eating at the same table, was inevitably lost.

The men I knew in Cognac were proud to be members of the "Army of General de Larminat," a unit of the regular French army largely composed of former members of the FFI, many of them veterans of the FTP. But there was also a pervasive nostalgia for the pure democracy of the maquis.

The town of Royan, once a favorite resort, was almost totally destroyed by allied bombs in January of 1945. The pocket was not liquidated until mid-April, in the last days of the war in Europe. The men I knew in Cognac did see full scale action at last. The 15 April infantry offensive of General de Larminat's FFI division was prepared by one of the largest air bombardments of the war, with more than 1300 Flying Fortresses and Liberators of the American Eighth Air Force dropping 460,000 gallons of liquid fire. The FFI division was reinforced by artillery, tanks, and colonial infantry of the regular French army and by units of the American 13th Field Artillery. Units of General Leclerc's French Second Armored Division smashed into the town on the evening of 15 April, dividing the well-fortified German pocket. Meanwhile the German positions were being shelled by destroyers. Fighting continued until 18 April when the last German troops surrendered. The French had 154 dead and 700 wounded; the Germans 479 dead. A number of prisoners were killed after the battle while working to destroy the 215,000 German mines.

Most of the civilians of Royan had been previously evacuated. When the firing ceased, about 350 civilians crawled from the ruins.

Glossary

adjoint Deputy.
Adjudant-chef Chief warrant officer.
attentistes They wait to see which way the wind is blow ing.
belote A game with a 32 card pack.
boches, fridolins, haricot verts, schleus Denigrative appellations for German soldiers. *Schleus* may derive from *schlass* (drunk) or *schliputer* (to stink).
bombonnes Demi-johns, large containers.
bon Ration ticket.
bouchées Delectable chocolates, at their best with soft praline filling.
café national An unpalatable substitute for coffee during the occupation.
carbonari Members of a 19th century secret society that fomented uprisings in Italy, Spain and France.
"C'était un jour de fête." "It was a holiday."
Charentaise A woman of the Charente (Cognac's) region.
confiseries Candy stores.
Darnand milice Joseph Darnand's was a semi-official, particularly repressive militia of 1943-4.
digestifs Cognac and Armagnac are among the best.
"Enfin!" "At last!"
épuration A "purifying" by identifying and punishing those who collaborated with the German occupier.
exode The flight south of civilians in June 1940.
Feldwebel Sergeant-major.

fille publique Prostitute.
Fra Diavolo *Brother Devil.* Romantic opera by Auber.
galons Stripes to indicate military rank.
Gemütlichkeit Cosy, mellow, good cheer.
Je suis seul ce soir I'm alone tonight (plaintive popular song).
jeune fille bien élevée A well brought up young lady.
Lycée Montaigne The author was a boarder in this school, fortunately for a very short time.
milicien A member of Joseph Darnand's militia.
napthalene Correct spelling *napthaline* (moth ball); a retired army officer recalled to active duty.
Offlag German prison camp for officers.
. . . oh oh OH, avec mes sabots! I stamp with my clogs! Refrain of a patriotic song.
Oradour-sur-Glane This village was destroyed and 634 inhabitants were shot in reprisal for the wounding of two SS troopers. One out of the 191 schoolchildren escaped.
Pinod (correct spelling: *Pinard)* Colloquial for wine.
P.L.M. A railroad line that also operated ships.
Printemps Large Paris department store.
"sans blague!" "No kidding!"
Soyez une bonne française Be a patriotic Frenchwoman.
Spahis Soldiers of the cavalry corps of the French army in North Africa.
von Rundstedt's small thrust The German counterattack stopped by the American army in the Battle of the Bulge.
Zouave A French infantryman of Algerian origin. His uniform included bloomer trousers and a tasseled cap.